JOURNEYS

Collected writings

Brixton and Bromley

South of the River Publishing

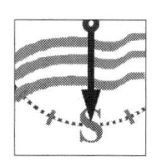

Copyright © 2021 Robert Williams

All rights reserved

The characters and events portrayed in this book are fictitious. Any similarity to real persons, living or dead, is coincidental and not intended by the author.

No part of this book may be reproduced, or stored in a retrieval system, or transmitted in any form or by any means, electronic, mechanical, photocopying, recording, or otherwise, without express written permission of the publisher.

ISBN-13: 9798585929595

Cover design by: Robert Williams
Cover photography: Robert Williams
Printed in Great Britain

*To the members of the writing groups in Brixton
and Bromley who have made this collection possible
and whose work is collected here.*

CONTENTS

Title Page
Copyright
Dedication
Introduction

CROSSING THE DOWNS Alison Bennett	1
MOUNTAIN Siobhan Reardon	2
LIFE'S JOURNEY Sue Evangelou	6
THE MICROCOSM THAT IS HOME HC Johnston	7
CATHARSIS Ana Castellani	10
ROBIN Cleo Felstead	11
FOLLOWING Robert Williams	27
BREATHLESS Tia Fisher	31
DESTINATION UNKNOWN Gwynneth Pedler	33
WELCOME ABOARD Carole Tyrrell	44
JOY'S JOURNEY Margit Physant	56
I'M GOING… Ana Castellani	59
ON THE LIST Dominic Gugas	60
MAY THE ROAD RISE Tia Fisher	62
PASSAGE Alison Bennett	75
TRAVELLERS' TALES HC Johnston	76
A THOUSAND KISSES DEEP Raymond Little	86

IT CAME Cleo Felstead	95
MOTHERHOOD WEEK 130 Cleo Felstead	98
MOTHERHOOD WEEK 182 Cleo Felstead	101
IN THE SYMPHONY OF LIGHT Ian D Brown	104
HUMAN LIMITATION Ana Castellani	116
A LIFE FOR A LIFE Robert Williams	117
WALKING THE BOUNDARY Alison Bennett	134
HOW SIGNIFICANT JOURNEYS HAVE IMPACTED MY LIFE Fay Brown	135
DIAMOND SHOWERS RE Charles	142
MOVING ON Alison Bennett	143
JOURNEYS HAIKU HC Johnston	145
ARRIVEDERCI PADRE Loraine Saacks	146
A NEWER PROMETHEUS RE Charles	149
THE TRYST Sue Evangelou	150
HIGH COMMAND CALLING – LOOPING THE LOOP Loraine Saacks	153
BEANS AND BULLETS Dominic Gugas	155
FADED PICTURES Ana Castellani	159
AN UNEXPECTED EXIT Gwynneth Pedler	160
ODE TO A CYPRIOT BEACH REVISITED Sue Evangelou	165
THE TIME TRAVELLER'S GOWN Trish Gomez	167
ABOUT THE GROUPS	194
ABOUT THE AUTHORS	195
THE PRODUCTION TEAM	201
Books In This Series	203

INTRODUCTION

Welcome, reader, to the second Brixton and Bromley anthology, where once again you will find the poetry, short-stories and essays of the two creative writing groups combined. The first anthology in the series, South of the River, was published in May 2019, and is also available on Amazon.

When we decided on the title *Journeys* for this anthology we didn't anticipate the journey we've all experienced this past year. But, despite the shadow that has blighted our lives, every writer in this collection has once again excelled themselves, pushing their art to new levels and proving that even in the worst of times when health, food, medicine, money and life itself are our main concern, creativity is also of importance. It is a nourishment we need more than ever, and is one of the many facets that make us human.

This time around, wishing to avoid the mistakes (and hard work) of editing the volume alone, I looked to some of the talented writers I have known for some time now to build an editorial team. First, I needed a leader, someone to pass the baton on to, so to speak, and Robert Williams kindly took this position. Robert has completed the majority of work on *Journeys*, from editing to compiling the contents to cover design and formatting, culminating in this marvellous book you are now holding, and is in title the Editor. Alison Bennett worked with poetry and prose and provided invaluable input on all stages of production from beginning to end. Carole Tyrrell concentrated her editorial efforts on the Bromley group's prose, and has also been instrumental in decision making from the start. I mainly took on editorial duties for the Brixton group's prose and poetry.

But, of course, the plaudits must go to the writers and poets of Brixton and Bromley: every one of them has something to say within these pages and they each do it in their own individual style. You will find journeys in every sense of the word here, be it physical, spiritual, metaphysical or existential. There is drama, comedy, time-travel, social comment, love and horror and so much more.

Read on, and thank you for accompanying us on this next leg of our journey; it's an interesting road and companions are always welcome.

Ray Little, 1st January 2021

CROSSING THE DOWNS
ALISON BENNETT

The road ahead is closed; we take the long way
crossing the Downs,
sun strong on autumn fields, trees turning, stray gulls.
Our cortege of two cars.

You would have loved this drive
through country where you ran your dog
when you were younger, more able.

Now we follow you,
not knowing when we will arrive,
not wanting the journey to end.

MOUNTAIN *SIOBHAN REARDON*

In a hilltop village in Morocco, with the sunset sparking and the air cooling, two tourists sit outside a café. They are the only strangers here and they are young and slim and brown and have casual clothes and unlined faces and a tourist guide to Morocco on the table in front of them. Clusters of men in their separate groups sit around them, taking them in, but no-one looks at them directly or smiles. And there is a kind of mirthless shrug when the woman gets up to call for coffee. It is delivered by a tall thin man who leaves their coffee on the table with a flourish and no word. She picks up on the atmosphere – she is the only woman here and she feels that she is not that welcome. She smooths back her hair and ties it in a topknot and thinks back to the bustling coffee shops of Fez, and women sitting with their children and their husbands, laughing, and groups of students sitting elbow-to-elbow eating those chilled pastries that made her mouth water, and she tries not to feel resentment towards her boyfriend who is too busy looking through his guidebook to notice anything.

In this little place atop a mountain where no tourist buses come, she sits and observes. The tiny town square. The old mosque. A scattering of shops – not many. And all about them those vertiginous views across the valley down to the plunging world below. And lastly, she thinks of the cool white hotel at the top of a huge flight of steps where yesterday they had wearily dragged their bags. After hours on those twisting dusty roads they'd almost cried with relief at the thickness of the walls and the coolness of the sheets. They had exchanged warm handshakes with the hotel owner, asked for nothing but water, shut the door and slept.

And now as they drain their coffee, there is suddenly some action in the square. They hear a loud hooting and honking – a din of dissent – and it is coming from a mule which is tethered outside a shop. Stolid, sun baked, his whole body braced with temper, he stands in the dirt and makes his objections. There is something slightly comical in the way he stretches out his neck and bares his teeth, and the girl looks on in sympathy. Is he thirsty? Neglected? He must have been standing there for hours in the heat. Nothing happens for what seems like a long time and the mule booms on, but then a man steps up, casually lifts a broken bath panel from an overflowing skip nearby, walks up to the animal and slaps it savagely across the torso with the full weight of it. The noise stops with a jerk. Nobody upbraids the man, nobody seems that interested – he just dumps the bath panel back in the skip and goes back to what he was doing. The tourists look on, mute with shock. Then they slowly begin to gather themselves and go, leaving coins scattered on the table. A young teenage boy in a baseball cap steps up.

"Would you like to see the mosque? You are not allowed to go in on your own, but, if you come with me, I will be your guide." He is very direct, and his English is very good, but they just want to get past him and go.

"Not now," they say, moving on. "Maybe tomorrow…" as they have learned to do.

***

At the hotel later that night they sit on the rooftop and eat lamb tagine laced with cumin and cinnamon and drink mint tea from long glasses – the tea tastes so green it makes their mouths tingle, and the food makes them groan with pleasure and stretch out their bare feet on the tiles. They eat quickly and silently. When they are finished, she mutters, "That was so good," and sits back, content and full.

They are the only people there. The hotelier has discreetly left them in peace. There is nowhere to go, no-one to share their stories with, no bar to enter, smiling. There is just the black night above them and that slight feeling of loneliness that tourists bring with them from other places. They are all alone in the world, muffled by their nowhereness. Below them in the tiny car park sits their dusty hire car, and above them are juicy white stars, teeming.

"So, I guess there's no mule protection league here then," he says, finally, trying to make light of it.

"Some chance of that 'round here!" she laughs, but her voice has a slight dip to it. And after a while, "Do you think we should have said something?"

"Like what? Unhand that mule immediately, my good man or I'll call the police!"

She gurgles with laughter at his impression of an English Toff, and then quickly, as if pulling herself up she says, "We really shouldn't mock."

"No, I know." And after a pause he hisses under his breath, "Coward." But he laughs when he says it and kicks her foot.

"What, I'm a coward? You're the one who works for a charity, so why didn't you do something?"

"Well, technically—"

"Technically what?"

"Well, technically, I'm in the charitable sector, but really I'm in IT."

"Can you hear yourself?"

"Loud and clear, person of extreme cowardice – and dirty feet!"

And they are happy again, high on a mountain and smug with love.

He flicks his wrist and the green numerals on his watch shine in the dark "You won't believe the time. It's still really early!"

"Don't tell me."

And, as they both stare off into space, there is the crackle and boom of a microphone being switched on, and a kick of static as the Imam begins the call to prayer. His voice is the voice of an elderly man and it rises in the night air, wavering and spooling out into the darkness like a lament until, just as suddenly, it stops.

The silence comes down again now, only thicker, and they shift in their seats. "Shall we go to bed then?" And she smiles in response and takes his hand and they walk down the winding staircase to their room where they turn on the giant fan above their bed to let the cool air swarm, drop their clothes on the floor and roll into each other's arms with lust and youth, boredom and relief.

LIFE'S JOURNEY *SUE EVANGELOU*

Life is a journey or so some people say,
Abide by the Signs, let them show us the way.
We'll Merge, we'll Give Way, we'll Bend to the Right,
When we stall at a Crossroads we'll dread the green light.
We'll Avoid Falling Rocks and a Slippery Road,
We'll stick to our Limit, we'll live by The Code.
Sometimes we'll Go Slow with No Overtaking,
Road Narrows Each Side, a time for some braking.
Sometimes we Stop, No Access ahead,
So we make a Diversion and leave the light that's red.
We Watch for the Elderly, we Do not sound our Horn,
We slow right down for Humps, we obey the Signs that warn.
We circle life's Roundabout and try not to make U Turns,
Foot down, straight ahead, time's not one of our concerns.
Sometimes the road is slow and hard, sometimes it's fast and clear
Yet now it seems that when we check the car behind is too near.
We speed up, leave it behind and round a Dangerous Bend
And all that's left in front of us is a Sign that says Dead End.

THE MICROCOSM THAT IS HOME *HC JOHNSTON*

In these times of occasional enforced solitude, or the monastic retreat which is so often presumed to be the best place for the creative writer, how may one journey in one's mind, if one cannot travel in three dimensions? "Oft have I travelled in the realms of gold, And many goodly states and kingdoms seen; Round many western islands have I been, Which bards in fealty to Apollo hold," as Keats put it. And who am I to argue with him?

During the early years of the French revolution, a young writer called Xavier de Maistre decided to study what was within his line of sight at home (which given the horrors outside, was understandable). He called his account "A Journey Around My Room". Each item is cherished, described, and given a history, and its emotional importance to the writer is recorded gracefully and lightly.

So let's try the exercise: the journey of a life, as shown in the chosen, meaningful artefacts that surround you every day.

Let's hope you haven't just blown a huge budget doing a "Kelly Hoppen", because anything new in taupe doesn't count. House rules. Actually, taupe doesn't count, new or old. Beige, maybe, at a pinch, if it's retro.

In my home, all seven continents are represented. You can take a trip around the whole globe just standing on my living room rug, which should be a big step up from an eighteenth-century Parisian's bedroom, no matter how much of an aesthete he was. Let's see:

Europe: Not counting the UK, as we are apparently now

on a different planet, the European representatives are a large multi-coloured glass fish (Murano, Italy), an inlaid marquetry sewing table which plays "Come Back to Sorrento" when you lift the lid, and some naked people in white marble resin, which were carried back with great effort from the family's Grand Tour a few decades ago. You have to place them carefully, where naked bums do not offend.

Africa: Engraved, incredibly heavy stone candlestick from Zimbabwe which doubles as a bludgeon against incautious burglars. A plate from Tunisia with some writing which may say "a present from Nablus" or possibly, "Allahu Akbar" or just maybe, "Death to the Infidel". (Same question over Chinese-script plates, ditto).

Asia: Well, there is the required dragon-with-pearl in gold embroidery on a table-runner (a table-runner? You put them on your dining table when you're giving dinner parties. It's a silk thing like a long scarf. Dinner parties? Oh, ask your gran). Then there's a Dog of Fo – a small stone doorstop – and two fake Tang horses in pottery standing guard on the fireplace. And a three-legged frog on a little enamel box, which is said to bring riches. At some future point, presumably. No waving cat, though, or goldfish.

Australasia: due to family connections, we are quite rich in Aussie artefacts, including a vivid blue plate sporting a bright green turtle, species unknown, and some sort of seed-head on which you drip eucalyptus oil to make the bathroom smell fresh. Well, differently pongy, anyway. And a porcelain platypus decorated with flowers in a Japanese Imari design, like you do.

North America: A stuffed Boston Terrier (not yer actual dog, a soft toy), in memory of a trip to Boston. My main memento of New York was a chipped tooth, and my take-away from Nashville is not to stay in a convention hotel, which are both hard to put on display.

South America: not been there myself but globe-trotting sister has, so I have a small tapestry antimacassar sporting a Mayan, and from further south I have the llama gourd. This is a dried gourd engraved with llamas and Peruvians, in which I keep a spare sewing kit. (Look, we're beyond asking "why" by now, surely?)

Antarctica: again, not a personal experience, although a friend did do the Ushaia thing, but I have a small family of china penguins (or a family of small china penguins) which is scientifically incorrect for Emperors but fits the china-buying public's expectations. Whoever they were. I inherited them. Or something.

So, there we have it.

I don't think Sir Joseph Banks or Elias Ashmole need lose any sleep over my cabinet of curiosities and there does seem to be an emphasis on "curious". When the far future version of Howard Carter breaks into the funerary chamber in which all my worldly goods have been stored for my journey to the afterlife (handily drawn out on my papyrus copy of the ceiling of the tomb of Rameses the Third, from Luxor), he may say, "Wonderful Things!" Or he may say "Where the hell did all this junk come from?" Both are equally valid.

Well, not quite equally.

Dear God, you know the biggest problem with all this? There is not a word of a lie. Not one word.

CATHARSIS *ANA CASTELLANI*

A place where echoes of my past will be unheard
Because of choice, not just because I'm far
I'd make new memories, I'd sing new songs
I'd reap uncovered meanings to take them all apart.
The whisper of my thoughts would all but disappear
I'd be lonely by choice, not lonely in my heart
The island is my stronghold, it's where I plant my trees
I'd watch them grow through mountains, reach different galaxies.

ROBIN *CLEO FELSTEAD*

Cast
Daniel – *late 40's, Londoner* (**V.O.** - Voice over)
Lee – *late 40's Londoner*
Mary – *70's Estuary accent*
Deborah – *early 40's. Estuary accent*
Jen – *40's Londoner*
Policeman – *30's Estuary*
Yute – *20's Londoner*
Newsreader – *Female. RP accent*
Presenter – *Male. London accent*

SCENE 1

'Rockin' Robin' by Michael Jackson plays but is interrupted by a pirate radio station playing drum and bass music. The sound of a heartbeat drowns out the music to a crescendo.

SCENE 2

The honking of a bus horn. Noise of city traffic. Daytime. Outside. Buses driving through slush in the distance, children playing in the background. Grime music coming from a nearby flat.

Daniel *(panting, then moaning in pain)* Argh ... I've fucked it Lee ... fucked it.

Daniel V.O. Lee found me. Shouted. Ran. Thank God he came down after all. I think ... yeah ... can't do this, I'm ...

Lee Alright mate, it's gonna be alright.

Daniel V.O. What's it all for, Lee? Too late now. I was just supposed to ... I didn't see it coming. I'm 48 years old, you don't get done for ... Knife cut through. Too late now. Too late.

Sirens pass in the background

Lee (*crying*) Dan, stick with it Dan. Don't bail out on me now.

Daniel V.O. Lee? You crying? (*Half laugh*) I've never seen you cry before.

Breathing. Silence.

SCENE 3

Fade up. Outside. Quiet. Bird song. Occasional noise of a car driving through slush in the distance. Sound of a heavy door being pulled open. Faint sound of classical music coming from inside.

Mary It's all white! All smooth and clean, like Ma's freshly made feather eiderdown. All smooth and clean. And there's Robin hopping along ... oh, this bloody door, (*straining*) it's so blooming difficult to ...

Mary strains, the door shuts heavily. Music can no longer be heard.
Mary (*sighs*) Gosh, it's bright out here. Oooo that's cold on my feet ... but the sunshine, the air! Wonderful. Feels wonderful. Dirt won't wash out, rub, rub, rub. Can't let Ma find these. Rub, rub, rub. Robin? Robin? Where's my Robin? Tweet tweet, bounce bounce. Hunting for food, looking out for danger. Left, right, left, right. Robin, come back! Where are you hopping to? Let me hop with you.

Creaking snow underfoot.

Mary Feet cold. Robin, Robin! Don't go away from me again Robin.

Sound of creaking snow underfoot. **Mary** *mumbles and mutters. Fade.*

SCENE 4

Outside. City traffic noise driving through sludge in the distance.

Daniel V.O. Jeeeesus! Is someone sitting on my chest? It hurts, heavy. Can't breathe. Snow on the ground soaking through, or is that blood? How's Lee? Still crying? Can't see his face, sun's in my eyes. (*Beat*) We aren't on the radio now are we, Lee? What would Khyro say about all this? "It's a kid's game, stay out of it, things aren't like when we were yute." Forget holy wars, this is Islington, and we are the forgotten children.

Loud noise of radio distortion. Outside. Top of a tower block. Sound of night traffic below. Some occasional shouting from a woman in a distant flat.

Lee (*straining*) There it is, it's come loose at the bottom. (*Reaching*) Got it.

Daniel Man, these kids were going mad for it. Like proper losing it. Then I dropped 'Messiah' and the whole crowd just went off. I love that feeling man, when the crowd are in your hands and the bassline just takes them away. I'm rushing just thinking about it.

Lee Pass me the wrench mate. Was that last week up at Kings Cross? York Way? Gutted to miss out on that one.

Daniel It was mental. Khyro wants to broadcast live from one on New Year's Eve. He reckons he can set up a transmitter at the party. Imagine that Lee! You think the DTI would be out on New Year?

Lee Don't think so, they won't be off their arses 'til mid Jan. (*Straining with wrench*) The aerial's bent but if I can just pull it back up …

Daniel Oh yeah, I never told you! Guess who was at the rave last week.

Lee Who?

Daniel Dawn Riley.

Lee Dawn? At a rave?

Daniel Yeah, Dawn Riley at a squat party. (*Laughing*) She didn't look impressed. She was with some chav bloke in a cap.

Lee (*playfully*) You're the one who went there, mate.

Daniel Shit man. That was at school.

Lee So, you wouldn't go there again?

Daniel Nah man, I'm on with Jen man. You know, she's sound. Things are good. What about you? Still seeing that squat girl? (*Teasing*) She started washing yet?

Lee Piss off! She's alright. Don't know. It's alright. She's pretty good on the decks. (*Beat*) Right I think that should be us back up and running.

*Sound of **Lee** dialling on a mobile phone. Muffled voice answers.*

Lee (*to phone*) Yeah Khyro, alright? The aerial was down but I got it back up. Wanna do a test?

Sound of radio distortion which tunes through to play some drum and bass.

SCENE 5

Radio tuning noise. Lands on classical music. Inside. Music lowers and continues in the background as scene fades up. Sound of out-

*going mobile phone ringing coming from **Deborah's** phone.*

Deborah (*calling out*) Mum? Mum?

Ringing sounds stops. A muffled voice answers

Deborah (*to phone*) John, Mum's not here. All her sheets were … so she'd been to bed but … she's not here.

Muffled voice replies

Deborah (*annoyed*) I've checked. The back door was locked. (*Pause*) Yes, the front door was shut. (*Pause*) I know it's heavy but she still could have opened it. She's even left the radio on. (*Switches classical music off*) Not like her. (*To herself*) Where are you Mum? (*To John*) She could freeze to bloody death out there.

Muffled voice through phone.

Deborah John. John! I don't know. I've called the police. Please. Come okay? Okay. Bye. (*To herself*) Shit!

SCENE 6

Outside. Quiet. Crunching snow underfoot.

Mary Hands are cold. Should be going back home now. Which way? Left, right, left, right. Robin, there you are! I see you, wait for me! I don't have wings to fly. (*Beat*) You were a beautiful boy. Perfectly formed. I can't believe you came out of me. Look at me now, this ragged old body, this beaten old flesh. I was so young. But there you were, a beautiful baby boy. You latched on straight away. You wanted me but you weren't allowed to stay. Not for long. A couple from Islington came. Mr and Mrs Rose I think it was. They looked kind. As they left, I heard them say they wanted to choose you a different name, Donny, David, something like that. What was it? Robin suited you so well. My Robin. I was told you had to go. No one gave me the chance to keep you. "What can you offer a baby?" the church women said. "Give him up and get on with your life." they said. So off you went. Off to Islington, miles from me. I cried for a year. I can't say they ripped you away from me but I was ripped apart, even though I let you go. I didn't have a choice, I hope you know that. (*Beat*) Little Robin. Helpless in the snow. Where have you gone? I know you're hiding. Bit steep round here. The snow's so fresh! I'm padding my way down, down, down the hill. Hands are cold. Where are my gloves? I must have left them in church, last Sunday, before I was showing, before the vicar knew. My gloves must be there.

SCENE 7

Outside. Sound of city traffic.

Daniel (*heavy breathing, moaning in pain*) Argh … Lee … I'm sorr … argh.

Daniel V.O. Our youth Lee. Those were the days. Before kids, before Jen even, before I grew up and stopped mucking about. Radio, raves, smoking, climbing towers, running from the DTI. We got away with it. We came good. Not this time though. I ain't making it through this one.

Daniel Lee … Jen … tell her …

Sound of sharp radio distortion. Scene switches to inside.

Daniel (*shouting to another room*) Jen, where are Isla's fairy wings?

Jen (*muffled reply*) They're in here under the sofa.

Daniel Mum'll get 'em sweetheart. (***Daniel's** phone vibrates*) Mum? Alright? How you doing? You okay? All set for Dad's tonight? (*Muffled reply*) No, no, I'm picking it up from the shop in a bit. They've done the 70 in silver but should be alright. (*Muffled* *reply*) Yeah, yeah, yeah, got it. (*Muffled reply*) Don't worry about that Mum, we got it covered. (*Sound of call waiting beeps on **Daniel's** phone*) Mum, Mum, Lee's calling, I'll call you back in bit. (*Answers call waiting*). Alright mate. (*A little hushed*) Yeah, all going ahead. Meeting him in the courtyard now. I've got to go pick up my Dad's cake for tonight but I can drop the cash round to you after. (*Muffled reply*) Nah, I got this, it's alright mate. (*Muffled reply*) I know, it's alright. (*More urgent muffled reply*) I don't want you to get involved, Lee … (*Forcefully*) Don't come down Lee, seriously. I've got this mate. I'll drop it to you later. (*Short muffled reply, **Daniel** calms down*) Alright. (*Beat*) You still good for my Dad's party tonight? Wicked, alright, laters.

Sound of loud radio distortion.

SCENE 8

Outside. Sound of creaking snow underfoot.

Mary Where are you Robin? What have you grown up to become? A man, a monster, a bird who hop, hops, hops through the snow? Okay, I'm playing. Oh, hide and seek! Yes. Coming ready or not.
Behind the bins? These aren't my bins. Hands are cold, feet are cold. Not my bins, not my village. No, Dad. I didn't think it through. Staff at the hospital told him to stop shouting at me. I never told anyone what really happened. They all thought I was a floozy. Lacking in true Christian values. The shame on our house! Having to tell the vicar so he could get me out of the village before I was showing. . How could I tell them? How could I say it out loud? I was so young, so naive. I should never have gone up to that flat … People warned me about him. That man. I had strong arms from lifting bales but he was a rower, I wasn't strong enough to stop him … I held him off for a long time though. My underwear got filthy dirty. I had to hide it from Ma. Rub, rub, rub. (*Short pause, bird song*) (*Determined*) You've run away good this time. I'll find you.

Footsteps in snow.

SCENE 9

Daniel *moans in pain.*

Daniel V.O. I left my flat whistling this morning. Excited. Feeling like I was on it. Shouting goodbye to my girls. My girls. Don't blame yourself Lee. I just … after all these years and it comes to this, lying in our courtyard, bleeding in your lap.

Lee (*Beat*) I should never have let you go and pick up, Dan. It was my mess. I should have sorted it. (*To **Daniel**, crying*) You stupid git.

*Sound of loud radio distortion with crackles. Scene switches to inside, sound of **Daniel** and **Jen** settling down in bed. The ruffling of a duvet, putting a watch in a drawer.*

Jen Did you hear Isla this morning? She woke up and said she'd dreamt she'd made friends with a gorilla!

Dan She's the monkey. Love that girl. Love you.

Jen Night darling.

They kiss. Noise of light switching off. Settling down. Short silence.

Dan Lee's lost his job you know.

Jen What? At the hospital?

Dan Yeah. His agency pulled him. Things are getting on top. He owes money to the Langford crew … (*Sighs*) It's not good.

Jen (*very awake*) Daniel Rose, what you thinking? I know you.

Dan (*beat*) Shift some stuff. Get a few things running, help him out.

Jen What?! Dan, seriously? No way. Not now we got Isla. It's not just us anymore, you know?

Dan I know, I know. I'm just thinking about it. A kid from Caledonian endz asked me to get him some gear. Five grand, Jen. Think about it. Sort Lee and we could go on holiday with the rest. Our first family holiday.

Jen Look, Lee's like family, I don't want to see him hurt, but not that Dan. You're 48 years old for fuck sake. Dealing is for kids. You're not some twenty something Islington bad boy anymore, you're a middle-aged husband and father. You grew up remember?

Dan Did I?

Jen (p*layfully*) Well ... maybe not. You have gone a bit grey though. (*Beat*) Please Dan. Don't freak me out. It ain't worth it, not anymore.

Loud radio distortion. Back to sound of city traffic.

Dan V.O. Jen, my beautiful Jen. You were always right.

Daniel (*weak*) Lee, look after my girls ... (*moans in pain*)

Lee You're gonna be alright Dan. That's not going to happen.

Daniel V.O. Do memories come with you when you're dead? What if I can't hold onto them? Isla dancing in her fairy wings. Jen's naked breast. My Isla. My Jen.

Daniel's *breathing becomes strained. The sound of sirens blaring through traffic.*

SCENE 10

Outside. Sound of crunching snow. The creak of a door opening.

Mary Ah, you are in the woodshed. This forgotten old body needs time to fold into shape. Ouch, splinters, just like the wooden benches in church, ripping my stockings. It's tight in here, in the pews. Holding in my tummy.

A siren can be heard in the distance.

SCENE 11

Outside. Car doors slamming shut.

Policeman (*approaching*) Are you Deborah? Mrs Hearn's daughter? I'm Officer Wright. How long has she been gone?

Deborah (*panicked*) I don't know, an hour? She could have gone out in the middle of the night. I don't know. I've knocked at the neighbours. They haven't seen her … she could have gone down the hill or the across the fields…

Policeman We'll look for her. (*Calling*) Spread out. (*To **Deborah***) Is there anyone one else she could be with? Other family members?

Deborah No, there's only me. I'm her only family.

SCENE 12

Daniel's *breathing becoming increasingly strained and wheezy.*

Daniel V.O. Why didn't I listen to you Jen? Will Isla even remember me? Will she even remember her Dad? I can't even think … I know how it feels, to not know where you come from, who you come from. I don't want that for Isla. I never thought it bothered me but now, here I am, losing my breath and I want to know. I want to know where I came from. (*Beat*) If I'd just listened to Jen … it was supposed to… how could I be so naive?

Radio crackles, loud and distorted. The honking of a bus horn. Noise of city traffic. Daytime. Outside. Buses driving through slush in the distance, children playing in the background. Grime music coming from a nearby flat, (the same track as in **Daniel's** *opening scene).*

Daniel Alright? Got my monies?

Yute Sure. You got my white? (*Pause*) I ain't handing it over 'til I see your tings blud.

Daniel (*noise of a coat zip opening*) It's all here, what you asked for. Where's my cash man?

Yute Don't think so bruv ...

Noise of a punch. **Daniel** *and* **Yute** *having a physical struggle.*

Daniel (*shouting out in acute pain*) Ahh.

Lee (*from a distance, shouting*) Oi, you fucker! Get off him!

Daniel (*groaning*) Lee?

Yute Old prick.

Sound of **Yute** *kicking* **Daniel**, *sound of a knife dropping to the floor and then footsteps running away.*

Lee (*running closer, out of breath*) Dan?

Daniel (*through pain*) He took the gear, Lee, I ain't got nothing. I fucked it mate. I've fucked it ...

Lee Shit Dan, you're bleeding ...

Daniel (*through short breaths*) I've fucked it mate ...

Long radio distortion noise. We hear **Daniel's** *breath, a strained wheeze.*

Daniel V.O. I'm glad you came Lee. You always had sense. At least we get to say goodbye. Leaving my girls this morning, I didn't know it would be my last. (*Beat*) She did. My birth mother. She chose to say goodbye. She gave her baby away. Me. How could she do that?

Daniel's strained wheezing becomes more laboured.

Lee Dan? Come on, man. Dan. Fuck. Dan.

SCENE 13

Sound of ***Mary*** *shivering. Inside the woodshed. A crow caws outside.*

Mary (*tired*) Robin, enough. I've reached the end of the game. "Forget me not," Ma said as I pulled away with Pa towards the mother and baby home. Miles to drive in the snow. I got terribly sick. Pa ranted and raved about me messing up the carpet in his Mercedes. 'Rockin' Robin' was playing on the radio. (*Beat*) I didn't mind it up there, with the other girls. They were kind. Ma and Pa didn't come, no one came, not once. (*Beat*) I can't feel my hands. Where are those gloves? My underwear's dirty. Rub, rub, rub. Can't let Ma find these. Rub, rub, rub. If I think hard enough, perhaps you will be delivered back into my arms. Then I could rock you and soothe you, be there when you feel all life's feelings.

SCENE 14

City traffic noise. ***Daniel's*** *breathing becomes a slow strained wheeze. A crow caws close by.*

Daniel V.O. Mum and Dad said she was very young. That she didn't have room for me in her family home. I never thought I was interested really but now ... I look at Isla and I see where she comes from. I see parts of me and parts of Jen. We're there. I want to look into her eyes, my real Mum, and see myself, find myself, somewhere in there. Here I am, dying in the snow, and suddenly I want to know. I need to know who you are

In the countryside.

Policeman (*distant but clear*) Mary! Mary! Maaaaary!

Mary (*exhausted*) Robin? You know my name!

Brief radio distortion.

Daniel V.O. Mum?

Mary (*struggling to voice*) Robin?

Daniel V.O. Mum?

Mary (*elated*) My son.

Daniel V.O. Mum, I … I …

Mary Robin, (*elated*) Robin!

Daniel V.O. Daniel. My names Daniel.

Mary Daniel. Yes. My Robin's name is Daniel. I've thought about you every …

Daniel V.O. (*interrupts*) Mum, where are you? I'm cold.

Mary Me too I'm cold too.

Daniel V.O. Call. I'll come find you. To be with you. Warm you up.

Mary I'd love that.

Daniel V.O. Call. As loud as you can.

Mary Alright. (*With effort*) Robin!

Daniel V.O. My names Daniel. Daniel Rose. Call that. I'm coming.

Mary Okay. Daniel Rose. I'm here!

Daniel V.O. Keep calling Mum.

Mary Daniel. Daniel Rose. My Robin. Daniel Rose.

Daniel V.O. That's it.

Mary Daniel. Robin. My Robin Daniel Rose.

Daniel V.O. That's it Mum. I'm coming.

*As **Mary** continues to call radio distortion drowns her out and turns into the sound of **Daniel's** wheezing breath slowing to a stop.*

Lee No, no. Dan. No.

In the countryside.

Policeman (*close*) Mary! Mary! Maaaary!

Mary Yes, I'm here, stuck in between the pews Daniel. I never wanted them to take you away. I always wanted to love you. I'm your mother. Hop. Hop to me my little Robin.

Policeman (*calling*) She's here!

Sound of a wooden door being pulled open.

Mary (*in a trance*) Robin, you came.

SCENE 15

Dark emotive drum and bass music plays.

Deborah (*calling off*) Sam! Turn that off! (*Music stops*) (*To phone*) Sorry Kel, bloody racket. Where was I? Yeah … The police found her round the back of 53, in their woodshed of all places. She only had her nightie on. Imagine being out in the snow like that! She was cramped up in the corner, her hands and feet had turned blue. Much longer and I think she would have … (*Sighs*) She was calling out this name over and over. Robin Daniel Rose. She keeps repeating it now, Robin Daniel Rose. Saying he's her son, that he found her in the snow. That he's my brother, to look under her bed for the records. (*Muffled voice from phone*) I don't know. She's never mentioned a Robin or Daniel before, let alone me having a brother! I'm going to get all her stuff tomorrow. I'll have a look then, I suppose. John isn't amused that she's living with us, as you can imagine. (*Laughs*) (*Sighs*) Anyhow, how are things with you Kel?

Conversation fades as upbeat drum and bass music rises in the background becoming a pirate radio broadcast.

Lee Renegade 107.5 locked on your dial. Bigging up all my North London crew. On the double six double nine. Hold tight my Islington fami …

The broadcast is cut short and becomes a lost signal. Radio tunes through to a new broadcast in progress.

Newsreader … asked the prime minister to formally apologise to the half a million women who were made to hand over their babies through forced adoptions between 1950 and the early 1970s. Young single pregnant women were sent to mother and baby homes during this time due to wide spread disapproval towards unmarried mothers. Many women have since come forward to say they were coerced into handing over their babies by "moral welfare officers" and church-run mother-and-baby homes. These vulnerable women claim they were not given information about the welfare services available to them, including housing and financial help. Many have suffered years of mental and physical ill health due to the trauma. The government rejected the demands for a public inquiry last August stating that lessons had been learned. Campaigners continue …

Radio tunes through to another station.

Presenter An ordinary man comes to a fatal end. It's a tragic story but I highly recommend getting a copy. Available in all good book shops from …
Radio tunes to a station playing the last few seconds of 'Rockin' Robin by Michael Jackson. Radio distorts. End.

FOLLOWING *ROBERT WILLIAMS*

"Are you sure you want to do this? I mean really sure. There's no going back," he said.

"Jack," I answered. He was the president but had insisted that I call him Jack. "There's always a way back. We just turn around." I was being flippant. We had made up our minds and wanted to be on our way.

"You know what I mean. There's a home for you here. By the time you decide you were wrong, there could be nothing to come back to."

"That could be good as well."

"You don't mean that."

I shrugged. Jack sat down, unwilling to give up the fight, and ran his fingers through his neatly parted hair. He looked every inch the nineteen-sixties poster-boy, from his penny loafers to his argyle sweater. Preppy. It was a passing fad. We were a long way from nineteen-sixty.

"Look, we've been through this before. All of us. We wanted a simpler life. A chance to raise our families in the sunshine, in the open air, to grow simple food with simple tools. We wanted to be away from the cities, the smog, the gangs and the crime. That's why we signed up for Homestead."

"But it was only a dream. You are still chasing a dream."

"It's a dream that's worth chasing. Real life just kills us." I looked out of the window at my feet just as the world beneath us drifted by. We were spinning slowly. It would be a few minutes before our rotation allowed the planet to appear in the window again. "Earth was killing us. That's why we decided to leave and go to Homestead."

"Knowing it would take you centuries?"

"Knowing it would take us centuries, yes. It was worth the wait. It was worth the risk. We knew that some of us wouldn't make it. Cold-sleep isn't perfect but most of us would wake up at our new home. A new world. Our lives could begin again. Better lives. We could plant crops and raise chickens. Breathe air that wasn't thick with smog."

"I'm sorry," he said. He really did look apologetic. A politician with morals. Unusual but it didn't matter. We had decided. We were going.

"Sorry? Why? It wasn't your fault."

"On behalf of Homestead then."

"It's not Homestead's fault or the fault of anyone living on it," I said. He relaxed a little after I said that. Homestead's media outlets had been trying to make the population feel guilty ever since we arrived. It was important for them to feel absolved. "If it's anyone's fault, it's whoever decided to send a faster-than-light ship to Homestead after we'd left. That ship left Earth decades after us but got to Homestead centuries before we arrived. No doubt the colonial board were chasing a quicker return on their investment. The bastards!"

He jumped visibly when I swore. I keep forgetting that this preppy world had gone puritanical. Swings and roundabouts.

"I'm sorry," I said. "But do you know how we felt when we arrived in orbit, expecting a new home, only to find a copy of the old one? In those centuries, you had taken the world we'd expected to farm and built the farms. Then the children of the farmers built towns around the farms and their children turned the towns into cities. By the time we arrived, you had taken Homestead and turned it into Earth."

"It must have been hard for you."

"Hard? It was fucking devastating." He jumped again. I didn't apologise. "We needed Homestead. *Our* Homestead. Not this." I gestured at the window but Homestead wasn't in view.

It had missed its cue. Typical. My timing was off yet again. "We were a ship full of disillusioned accountants retrained as farmers arriving at a world that wanted graphic designers. We felt useless."

"We could find you places in our society."

"Doing what? We can't farm here. There is no land that isn't taken up with cities or automated robo-farms. And we can't go back to our old jobs. Our skills are centuries out of date. We are useless."

"You're not. Some of your people have decided to settle."

"They've given up. They've seen their dreams ripped away and daren't dream again."

"They will be retrained. We can give them a good life here."

"Good luck to them, in that case, but the rest of us want to move on. You know we have some of your people as well?" We had filled our spare spaces and could have filled another two ships with the people who had approached us.

"Of course. We wish they – and you – weren't going but we support you and hope you find what you are looking for. I hope you understand we had to give it one last try to persuade you to stay. You are all taking such a huge risk."

I nodded. "Thank you for that. And thank you for the upgrade. The new engines will let us get further away and hopefully we will find a world that isn't already settled."

"We've given your ship a few likely candidate worlds and trained her in faster than light flight. Sandy is a quick study."

She had shown me some of them earlier. All the worlds looked very promising and were thousands of light years away. We would be undisturbed. I was sure of it.

The ship's rotation, which had been steadily slowing, stopped and I found myself starting to float. Jack made his way to the airlock.

"You know where we are if you change your mind."

"We won't but thanks."

He waved and I closed the door, watching as his ship

moved away from the *Sandman* and started on its way back to the surface.

"Sandy?" Our ship's voice and persona were female. Calling her Sandman would have been stupid.

"Yes, captain?"

"Set course for the first world on the list and prepare my sleep pod."

"Yes, captain."

"Are you sure you are familiar with the FTL engines?"

"Yes, captain. I have had several trial flights over the last few weeks. I am confident I will get you to your new home."

Our old engines had taken us over three hundred years to make the trip from Earth to Homestead. The new engines could take us back to Earth in thirty minutes but we weren't going there. We would be sleeping for another few years while Sandy flew us faster than light. Hopefully, our target world would be empty when we arrived. If not, we'd fly on.

"That's good enough for me. Let's go."

BREATHLESS *TIA FISHER*

The summer before the wind blew change across the world
we picnicked in your garden as the heat haze rose & swirled in
heavy fumes above the Alentejo fields, gasping at the air
that sun had simmered clean of oxygen
gathering up the flowers, fletches twisting
as slowly as their name fell from my tongue
    calêndula
    not *calendar,*
      you laughed
your low rumble-of-tyres-on-tarmac laugh
before you put me on a plane, those seeds
pressed into pots like promises passed in the terminal
you told me all I had to do was wait—but
don't hold your breath you said, &
I rolled *espere* in my mouth
as sour as lemon drops,
watched the ground below me
    fall away,
    watched
    all winter
as the earth froze under snow's white chickens
brooding on the rows of terracotta pots outside my sill
    & still
    you couldn't, wouldn't come:
you watched the news & held your nerve
& even when the seeds kept faith by greening into sparks
you made the game of chicken last
until last chance had shut the window
    tight—

so tight
you said you
couldn't
    breathe.

DESTINATION UNKNOWN
GWYNNETH PEDLER

The motley line of children, some with school hats pulled down over their brows, trudged on. Passers-by stopped to watch, some calling out Good luck or God Bless, and bus drivers waved and gave them a thumbs up, but the silent children moved steadily on as if in a dream. Now and then the silence was broken by cries of "I want me Mum," but there were no warm, comforting arms to be found. Most were gripping a small case which they shifted from one hand to the other and others had bags dangling from their arms, while a few clutched brown paper parcels tied up with string. Everyone had a cardboard box hanging over their shoulder.

This winding line gave the appearance of a colourful snake slithering through the undergrowth. A sudden shout of "stop" halted their progress. Those brave enough lifted their heads and looked around at the familiar streets that had been their playground for as long as they could remember, but the majority stared at their feet, afraid of what they might see. A quavering voice called out "where are we going?" and received the curt reply "wait and see." They trailed up the unfamiliar hill, where neat, clipped hedges, colourful flowers and crisp white net curtains hung at the windows. It was nothing like their beloved streets, covered in chalked hopscotch grids, abandoned skipping ropes and friendly corner shops.

They came to a train station and went down to the platform where hundreds of other children were huddled together; there was an unusual subdued hush, an air of despair so unlike

East End children as they were jostled about, and even more children arrived after them. The sound of a steam engine and the earthy smell of coal fumes changed the mood of the children. A ride in a train was something only experienced on Sunday School day trips to the sea. But it was short lived. Even the sight of the blazing fire in the driver's cab or the coal blackened fireman was not enough, and the excitement was quenched like candle in a breeze.

After a while, eyelids began to droop, and little heads nestled for comfort into each other's shoulders. The steady rhythm of the train as the wheels bumped over the sleepers soon worked its magic; the diddle dah diddle dah acted like a gentle lullaby, bringing beautiful peace into a day that had been filled with fear, uncertainty and loss.

With a great deal of clanging and screeching the train drew to a halt. One by one the children opened their eyes to loud voices echoing along the platform, and the crashing of carriage doors. "Get out, hurry up, there are more trains expected."

Gathering their cases, their eyes still glazed with sleep, they stumbled down the steps and stood in their little group, huddled together like a family. When every carriage was empty the train rumbled away, leaving behind groups of bewildered children like a collection of lost souls waiting in silence. At last they were led along the platform to the waiting coaches. No excited chatter or calling out to friends; gone were the days when authority was challenged. As the coach moved away, glimpses of country wildlife and sweeping green fields could not arouse any curiosity in the children's' wearied minds. They just wanted to go to bed, and clung to the words, "Never mind, you will be home by Christmas." These words were a lifebelt in a raging sea. One by one the coaches drew up and deposited the children before setting off to fetch more. They had arrived at their destination but more separation was imminent as they were divided into school groups. Any companionship formed during this stressful day was abandoned. Friends were reunited, the familiar faces of their teachers a comfort. The day had reached an acceptable end, if not a particularly desired one.

As the children gazed at the empty, quiet streets, the only sounds that could be heard were their gasps. The pretty painted houses were like ones they had only seen in picture books and not a bit like their red brick neighbourhoods, full with the bustle of traffic, noisy children and barking dogs. The striking of the church clock was the only thing that connected today with yesterday. It was a ghost town, deserted, abandoned and unloved. The teachers marshalled them into school groups towards a large single storied building in the middle of the square. Once inside, the bustle and chatter and the smell of food came as a surprise. A comforting feeling crept over them and for the first time during that long day they relaxed as the adults reassured them with their friendliness.

A plump man made a speech of welcome and explained that the people in the room were going to invite them to their homes until the war was over. One by one the children were chosen. How terrible that sounds, as if they were cattle being sold at auction. The last adult departed leaving a number still to be billeted. The children moved closer together as if forming a barricade, the feeling of insecurity overwhelming them, and some began to whimper. These unchosen few were once more led out onto the square where farm lorries were standing waiting to take them to cottages further into the country. Still clutching their precious belongings, they climbed onto the lorries. At their destination, the teacher jumped off first and called out "one of you out here please." A girl stood up, waved to her companions and jumped down. She turned and looked at the two small, isolated farm cottages. A lump rose in her throat as a tear traced its way down her face. She felt abandoned, never before had she felt so lonely, so helpless, so friendless. The sound of the lorry faded away and the silence engulfed her. Christmas seemed a long way away. She looked towards the cottage where she saw two pairs of hands waving to her. With a friendly hug, the door was closed, and she was drawn into the house. She had arrived.

The table was covered with a sparkling white tablecloth and dainty cups, saucers and plates, while in the middle was a large jam and cream cake; it looked like a birthday treat which made her feel special, but at the same time it brought memories of home. Her eyes scanned the room; it looked like pictures she had seen in her reading books at school with its tiny window with pretty flowery curtains, and inglenook fireplace. Two elderly people sat companionably on either side of the fire.

Later, with the lamp lit, they talked about their lives. She told them her father was a stevedore and worked at the docks. As she spoke, she wondered what they would be doing at home and whether they were missing her. They told her they had worked at the local farm, he as a shepherd, she as a cook and they had no children. She wondered how they would cope with a young girl and hoped she would not disrupt their peaceful life too much. Now it was time for the tour of the house, and she was in for a big surprise. Many of the comforts she had in London were not on offer in rural living. The water supply was one tap in the kitchen, all cooking was done on the fire, the only toilet was in the garden along a stony path, toilet paper was squares of newspaper, and lighting came from lamps and candles. There were plenty of new things to learn and it seemed to her that living in the country must be very hard work. Each of them held a candle as they climbed the steep wooden stairs to her bedroom. What a surprise to see how neat and tidy it was, not a bit like home where the floor was often littered with books, paper and games. Mrs. Parker picked up a china jug that was standing in a large bowl and explained that all water must be carried upstairs, and she would need to wash in her room. She was exhausted and ready for bed, and after her host said goodnight, she stepped into the room with thoughts of the day crowding her head. She sat on the edge of the bed and wept until, still in her clothes, she fell asleep.

Next morning, she opened her curtains and gazed upon a garden full of fruit and vegetables, a greenhouse and an orchard. Why hadn't she noticed this last night? She longed to explore and hoped she might be allowed to grow something. That really would be something to write home about. The small patch at the back of the garden back home was devoted to the boys' football pitch. But there were no boys to claim ownership here. If she was going to stake a claim to a corner she needed to tidy herself up and go down to breakfast. The tempting smell of bacon drifted up the stairs and her tummy rumbled at the thought of food. She called out a cheery Good Morning as Mrs. Parker emerged from the kitchen, covered from head to foot in a voluminous overall. Bacon at home was a special treat on Sundays, but here she was on a Saturday being offered a whole plate of it. She gazed round expecting to see Mr. Parker sitting by the fire but the room was empty. On the table sat a large loaf of bread. This was all so different from home, she was confused and uncertain; in London her mother gave each of them a slice of bread and butter, so should she wait to be given the bread or was she expected to take what she wanted? Her host came in with a cup of tea and told her to cut herself some slices.

There was so much she would have liked to write in her postcard to her parents, but in the end, she just told them she was happy. Holding the card tightly she set off to find a postbox and seemed to have walked a long way. She trudged on, hoping someone would tell her where the postbox was, but the only sign of human activity was the noise of a distant tractor. Suddenly her attention was drawn towards a clump of brightly coloured poppies; she knew they were poppies because she had seen pictures of them in books at school. As she bent down to look, a bee settled onto the flower; it was fascinating to watch as it fed itself on the nectar before flying away. Now, having enjoyed the poppies, the journey became more interesting as she noticed other flowers and the number of different ones awakened her imagination and she began noticing how many different colours there were. Maybe, she thought, the country could be interesting, but how much better if her friends were with her and even better if her mother were there. Her mind wandered to them and hoped they were happy. Her best friends

Marguerite and the twins Iris and Lily had still been on the lorry; how near were they and was it possible for them to meet? She came upon a postbox at last, and, mission completed, she turned around and made the journey back. Never mind, she thought, tomorrow she would meet her friends outside the church in the town where they had been told to meet.

She jumped out of bed next morning eager to get on with the day. The road to town was straight, no problem with getting lost, no busy roads to cross, no pavements just hedges each side, but the lack of traffic made it very safe. The road seemed never ending until a few houses appeared at last, but where were the people she wondered? As she was turning this over in her mind several doors were thrown open, and people rushed out shouting "we are at war, Winston Churchill has just made an announcement." Her heart missed a beat, and she quickened her step, wanting to get near to the people she knew. The church was surrounded by crowds of chattering children and she searched among them for her friends. At last she found Marguerite and the twins. They told her they were staying on neighbouring farms quite far from her house, with the journey to school quite different, and that weekends would prove impossible to meet up. However, Marguerite came up with an idea. There was a house near the cottage where she was billeted, and she suggested they ask their teacher if he could arrange for her to move there. They set off to find Mr. Kingsley and put the idea before him. All three looked at him with pleading eyes, and he promised to look into it. The teachers announced that the children were to share the school with the local pupils, attending for half-days each. The school looked like a large shed, single story, small, white and surrounded by grass. They went inside and began to explore; everything was there but on a much smaller scale. The tour ended, sad goodbyes were said, and once more she was on the long journey home. How she would love to tell her mother all that had happened, hear her say "you did well, little one."

At the end of the week the good news arrived; she would

be moving to the cottage near to Marguerite at the weekend. It was a large ramshackle house, and it couldn't have been more different. No neat and tidy room, and the three, not too clean, small children gazed at her as she carried her case inside. Her host burst into the room shouting, "I'm Pam, these are my children, Tommy, Sissy and Milly, who are you?" Introductions completed, they all went upstairs, and she was introduced to her bedroom. How could anyone gather so much stuff around themselves and still find room for a bed? It was a good job she hadn't brought much as there were no cupboards or drawers to keep the room tidy. But the atmosphere was one of happiness and relaxation. That evening after a delicious dinner they read to the children until they fell asleep. She never discovered where all the bedrooms were, nor how they all fitted into them. The bathroom was in an outhouse; how relieved she was to find there was a bath with running hot water although the toilet was, like the previous one, at the bottom of the garden.

The following morning, she set off with Marguerite for school, arm in arm, chattering away just as they had in London. They ambled along picking up grasses and chewing the sap. They had already turned into country children without noticing it, but by Friday they had had enough of the journey. The weekend was in sight though, with exploring to do. Her host seemed very happy for her to go out and gave no orders about coming home. The girls had been warned about the deep well further along the lane so naturally their first stop was the well. They leaned over and dared each other to lean further each time. At last, they took notice of the warning they'd been given about never getting out if you fell in and took to throwing in stones to see how long it took them to hit the water. They wandered further up the lane, jumping over ditches. With so much activity and the warmth of the sun tiring them, they lay down on the grass and looked at the blue sky and puffy clouds. They began giving names to the various clouds, giggling happily, two friends helping each other to forget the war, their family and London for a short time; true friendship born out of tragedy.

At breakfast the next morning, Bert came in to announce that as the weather seemed set the threshing machine would arrive later that day and work would start first thing in the morning. They wandered down to the golden field, where the sound of heavy feet and loud voices heralded the arrival of the labourers. What should they do? Were they allowed in the field? They had no experience to draw on and crouching with their arms round around each other they waited. They were used to their local bobby at home telling them off for minor misdeeds, but this was a very different offence; would it call for stricter punishment? The voices began to get softer, and finally died away. Peering out the scene was empty, escape was possible, and they took it, tearing along the road to the safety of home.

The bright Monday morning heralded a day just right for harvesting. The house already had an air of business around it. It was absolutely necessary for the corn to be threshed in the next three days because the machine was due to go to the next farmer after that. Speed was of the essence and the burly men responded with alacrity; their take home pay depended on it, they knew the farmer would pay a visit several times a day to check their progress. This seemed too good an opportunity to miss but today was a school day and it was their week for afternoon lessons. Marguerite arrived dressed ready in her school uniform, with her school bag over her shoulder and they set off on the long walk to school. The sound of the threshing machine roused their excitement and their steps slowed. They looked at each other, both with the same thought in mind. They could always run to school. And so, it was the beginning of truanting. Although they didn't realise it, they would never set foot in the school again. The field was full of men shouting, others running about, sweat covering their bodies. She thought of her father and the stevedores at the docks and for a moment wished she was there, but the excitement gripped them, fascinated them, they were caught up in the drama. They crept nearer, trying to keep out of sight but drawn towards the scene. They jumped and turned as a hand grasped their shoulders and a loud voice shouted, "What do you think you are doing?" He quick-marched them to the labourers. "Oh, they are all right, they are evacuees, let them stay."

They became an accepted part of the scene with full attendance rights. Wives arrived with their husband's lunches, work stopped, they all sat down to eat. They were plied with chunks of bread and cheese and pickled onions, all washed down with a flask of tea. They munched away. This really was an adventure. School was forgotten, this was fun.

Once harvesting was over, they looked for fresh ways of spending the day with no thoughts of school. The weather was getting colder, the days were shorter and as it was now October, they knew the chances of mooching about at will were drawing to a close. Weeks had gone by, but no one mentioned school. She was unaware of rationing as she had good meals and never questioned the source until the morning she was asked to help prepare the food and was shown an un-plucked chicken. As far as she knew chickens came minus their feathers but that was in the past. Pam showed her how to do it. It was really hard work but the praise from Pam when the task was finished made her proud, and later when they sat to eat it her heart swelled with pleasure. A few days later she was invited to watch Bert skin a rabbit. Her next job was to pluck a beautiful pheasant. Further surprises were in store; pigeons were plucked and put into a pie. There were plenty of pigeons in London and they were looked upon as a nuisance, so she had no guilty feelings about pigeons, and it became obvious to her that Bert was a night poacher. No wonder they fed so well. One day a new evacuee called Kitty arrived. The weather had turned, and Kitty always seemed cold, especially her feet, so they huddled together on the settee in front of a roaring fire. She was a very sad figure, thin with wispy long hair and a worried expression on her face. Her feet were covered in painful chilblains which Pam covered with cream every day. The children would huddle up and never tire of listening to the same stories every day. It was a happy and loving home.

One morning the postman called with a letter from her mother who was coming to visit the next Sunday. She jumped and shouted the good news all over the cottage. Her father had visited once or twice, coming with the school coach that came every two weeks and, though it was good to see him, this was her mother, the one who cuddled and kissed her, comforted her when she was sad. When the day came, she was up early, wandering from room to room and looking at the clock. Mother arrived at last, with hugs and kisses. Country life had been good, she had learned a lot, but now, in her mother's arms, she longed for home, for her room, for all she still loved, the chipped plates, the mug with Paddington Bear on it. After dinner she took her mother to her room; little did she know the surprise that her mother had in store for her. She held her hand and broke the news. "You are coming home," she said. Had she just dreamed that? She glanced at her mother's face and knew it was true. There was a look of joy on her Mother's face too. They flung their arms around each other, hugging and crying with joy. At last when they had calmed down her mother explained how this had come about. Her aunt had found an empty cottage in a small village outside a big town, negotiations had taken place, and from January they would be able to rent it. There would be room for her grandmother and great aunt, and her father when he was not working. It sounded bliss. Arrangements were made for a school and she wondered if her parents knew she had not attended for months. She was to spend Christmas here and go home in January; first she would stay with her father in London until her mother had settled in, then her new life would begin. It would still be in the country, but her family would be with her, and anyway she knew about country ways now. She rarely met Marguerite as the days were short and the weather very cold, but when her mother had gone she rushed to give her the good news, expecting Marguerite to be as excited as she was, so it came as a surprise to see her burst into tears, and they both cried. They had been very good friends to each other when they had most needed it and would miss each other. They dried their eyes, hugged, laughed, cried then once more burst into laughter.

Christmas was fast approaching, and Pam had recently been shopping and brought back a huge amount of paper chains for them to make ready for Christmas. Marguerite and little Jimmy were invited to join in the fun and the cottage was filled with noise and laughter over the next few days, all thoughts of the sad goodbyes to come far from their minds. Clapping and cheering echoed round the cottage as Bert hung up the paper chains and pictures the children had made. She sat down at the decorated table where a turkey took pride of place, an enormous one like she had never seen before. Bert had been very busy it would seem. Later, good friends from a nearby village arrived adding to the merriment already taking place and singing and dancing began until at last she crept off to bed. She would soon be saying goodbye to this life, but she would never forget it.

The teachers had lost track of how many pupils were still living in this small town as week by week parents had arrived to take their children home. London was safe; this was a phoney war and they wanted their children home where they belonged, and now, she was going home too. To a new beginning, new experiences, and new friends, but she would never forget Marguerite.

WELCOME ABOARD *CAROLE TYRRELL*

It was as the doors slammed shut that Phil remembered the trains weren't supposed to be running over the weekend.

"Sorry mate," he mouthed to the blurred pale face looking in through the doors. Phil could hear him frantically pushing the open button from outside before thumping on the doors and giving him the finger. But the train had begun to move off and he was soon lost to sight. Phil walked away from the doors and looked for a seat.

"Not so crowded on here as usual," he muttered. "Must be my lucky night." The train had stopped at the station when it shouldn't have done and Phil blamed the engineering works. The evening had got off to a good start.

It was one of the Thameslink trains with no divisions between coaches and, as he looked down its length, he couldn't see any other passengers. He shook the raindrops from his once carefully gelled hair and unzipped his jacket.

"At least my shirt's stayed dry." Phil removed his damp jacket and shook it carefully before draping it over the back of a seat. The new shirt would result in another letter from his bank about his lack of finances but appearance was everything with his mates from work. "Nice and toasty on here!"

He sat down and took his phone out of his pocket. Phil thought about the lads already getting the drinks in and how little he wanted to go out tonight. But after drinking themselves into Dutch courage, they'd all be off to prowl the streets of London, the bright lights, the noise, the crowds, all smiling and glittering with that sturdy optimism that this Christmas would be different. He scrolled down his messages and then started to watch football. The outside world went past in an impressionistic blur as he briefly glanced out of the window to see where he was. Phil put his phone down on the seat beside him, fumbled in his pocket for the can of Red Bull he'd brought with him and popped the ring pull.

"It's going to be a long night, need to keep my strength up," he raised the can to his lips. As he paused in his drinking, he gave out a huge belch.

"Sorry, fellow passengers." he shouted and almost giggled. Then his phone vibrated, and he picked it up. A text awaited him from an unknown number.

Welcome Aboard! Nice 4 us to be travelling 2gether. Smiley face emoji.

Phil looked around. He still couldn't see anyone, and he rolled his eyes.

"Customer care crap. Next they'll wanting my feedback." He deleted it and continued drinking.

We want you to enjoy your journey so just sit back and let us do the driving. Smiley face emoji.

"Yeah, a lovely journey through the backside of Sarf London on a rainy night." Phil deleted this text as well. The train was picking up speed as the driving rain battered against the windows.

"Wha...!" he started and spilled some of the drink. A blast of cold air suddenly blew on him from nowhere. "It was lovely and warm when I got on," he thought. Phil stood up, still holding his can, and looked around as he shivered. As he did so he felt the phone vibrate. The text awaited him.

Not too warm for you now? We like to look after our customers. BTW it's not healthy drinking those energy drinks. Sympathetic face emoji.

He looked around again.

"Who is this?"

A friend. Smiley emoji.

Phil texted a reply. *Stu if this is you, I'm gonna kill you. Not funny. Is this your idea of a joke?* Angry face emoji.

Puzzled face emoji from Stu.

Ok, ok if that's how you want to play it. C U soon, Get the beers in. Several smiling face emojis.

He held the phone in his hand as he continued to swig his Red Bull. "Can't read any of the station signs. Where are we?" he muttered to himself as he looked out of the window.
But there was nothing but darkness and, as he returned to the screen, he thought that he saw someone behind him peering over his shoulder. He jumped and looked around as a prickle of fear travelled up his spine.

Don't worry you're not on your own. I'll keep you company. Smiley face emoji.

"That's enough! Keep your stupid texts to yourself!" he glared down the length of the train. But it was still empty and he was relieved that it was beginning to warm up again. A video appeared on the screen and, as he prepared to rant into it, he saw that it was from Georgie. He was raising a glass, a string of tinsel was around his neck and he was wearing a Christmas jumper. It featured a bondage clad elf and the slogan "I've been very naughty this year Santa – it was much more fun!" Stu, Dan, Justin, and Mark's heads all bobbed into frame, their faces flushed and the collection of empty and half empty glasses on the table demonstrated that the evening was in full swing.

"Come on! Where are you, man?" shouted Stu. In the distance behind them a group of revellers had formed themselves into a conga line which was dancing around the pub. A paper party hat appeared from nowhere and drifted down to land on top of the glasses. Phil smiled wryly. Everyone knew what London was like at Christmas. Gaggles of office workers moving in small flocks around the streets, completely stuffed and merry from their Christmas lunches, the girls teetering on high heels in their Christmas best but not ready to go home yet.

"I'm on the train. Be with you all soon!" he said into the phone. They all cheered and raised their glasses.

"Last one here buys the Christmas dinner!" shouted Stu.

"We've booked it in your name!"

"He must be taking the long way round!" joked Darren. "The scenic route."

"Is there one round Sarf London?" said Dan determined to have the final word. A bunch of plastic mistletoe suddenly appeared on the screen.

"Get lucky, boys," said Phil smiling determinedly.

"Sorry mate, the conga's coming our way!" the picture vanished, and the screen was blank again momentarily.

Shame you can't be with your friends, but it looks as if they're getting on fine without you. Smiley face emoji.

Phil threw the phone onto the seat, smiled to himself grimly and muttered under his breath. "You like to play, do you? Well, so do I." He looked down the carriage to the first toilet which was one of the circular ones where the door opened like a fan. It was closed. Phil loathed them. He'd been in one once when, without warning, the door had suddenly opened and revolved around to display him sitting on the toilet to a packed train of commuters. But it was a perfect place to hide, he realised. Phil smiled exultantly.

"Ready or not? I'm coming to find you!" he announced.

The reply was instantaneous.

Oh puh-lease! Frowning face emoji.

The train suddenly stopped. Phil peered out of the window. "There's nothing out there!" he sat back again, "No lights, nothing, surely we should be almost at London Bridge by now." Suddenly, he needed to see the Millennium Wheel, Christmas lights in the Strand, the Christmas tree in Trafalgar Square. He drained the last of the Red Bull and crumpled the can throwing it down on the carriage floor.

Ready or not here I come! Smiley face emoji.

The text scared him.

Behind you! Smiley face emoji.

"What?" he looked around as the lights in the train began to go out, one by one, carriage by carriage and the dark advanced towards him. He began to move further up the train as the darkness pursued him. As he passed the last toilet, he heard a sound behind him. The door had suddenly and stealthily begun to open. "I'm not going to look," thought Phil as the now inevitable text pinged.

I thought that you wanted to play. Sad face emoji. Phil hit delete.

Suddenly, he just wanted to run, run away. "Who are you? What do you want?" Then the final light went out and his back was up against the driver's door. As his eyes adjusted and some light came in through the windows, he could see that the toilet door was now fully open and looked like a dark doorway ready to swallow him. "I wish I'd never got on this train." Phil thought bitterly. As he stood there, he could hear the other two toilet doors further down open.

"Where are you? Where are you hiding?" Phil growled as he stalked through the carriages opening and closing all the toilet cubicles, looking under seats and on luggage racks as the train began to move again. He threw open the door to the first-class section, looked under seats and tables, and then stood in the middle of it and raged.

"Where the hell are you, you bastard?"

There was a sliver of light coming from under the door to the driver's cab and he almost ran towards it. "So, you're in there, are you?" he banged on it with his fists. It remained shut. "Come out I know you're in there!" he screamed as the train flew through another station with a whoomph of air and lights. Then with a swish and the sound of locking doors all three of the toilets on the train opened and shut loudly in unison. He turned and began to bang on the driver's door again. "Let me in! Let me in! Let me sit in the cab with you!" Phil pleaded. "I've got money I can pay you! Please!" He stood back, breathing heavily, and waited for a response.

A text appeared and he groaned.

There's nobody there. Sad face emoji.

"I don't believe you! Someone's driving this train!" Phil continued to bang on the door until his hands hurt. "Bastard!

I'm going to report you! You won't get away with this" Breathing heavily he almost threw himself down on a seat. The only illumination was the screen on his phone. He didn't want to hold it up as he was scared of what he might see. "Supposing the battery runs down and leaves me in the dark." he thought.

But you won't be alone. You'll have me to keep you company. Smiley face emoji.

Phil deleted it and shoved the phone back in his pocket. He looked up at the illuminated information board indicator suspended from the ceiling in the carriage and gasped. The loading indicator screen's colour coded symbols showed that every carriage was full.

But if I'm not company enough for you. Angry face emoji.

"But there's only me on here! Why is it saying that it's full?" Suddenly, an elbow poked him in the ribs making him start. There was an aroma of stale aftershave and perfume, hamburgers and food beginning to waft around. "Oww!" a stiletto heel pressed down on his foot. He winced. There was a rustling of paper and a monotonous thumping of music almost next to Phil's ear.

"I'm on the train!" a man loudly brayed.

Phil knew that he was no longer alone. The crowd of passengers were jostling him, pushing him, a backpack thudded into his face, and he felt himself being jostled by invisible passengers wanting to sit down. He shrank back against the carriage wall. Phil's face was pressed up against the window, his ribs were beginning to hurt, he was half twisted round, his arms around his head. But there were more and more of them trying to sit on top of him and making him stand up to move away from them. Now he was trying to step over bags and feet and backpacks as they all seemed to want to trip him up.

"I can't breathe!" he thought and started to try to push his way through to the doors where he hoped that there might be some air. A wave of non-existent people, elbows jabbing making Phil turn this way and that to try and avoid them, the smell of closely packed commuters filling his nostrils and making him want to gag.

"I'm on the train!" the voice shouted again.

"Shut up!" screamed Phil and the noise of people became louder. The crowd were pushing and shoving and manhandling Phil until his back was against the doors. He was trapped as slowly they began to open. "No, no don't do it!" Phil screamed sweat making his once pristine new shirt cling to him as cold air and rain began to come in behind him. He reached vainly for the close button as he felt the doors opening wider behind him as the train sped along. He started to try and push his way through, but the imaginary commuters were solid. "Move you bastards, move!" He shoved and kicked but was thrust back again. There was more cold air was coming in behind him as the doors opened wider. Phil quickly saw the handrail by the door, grabbing it like a drowning man, managing to push his body through the crowd out of sheer desperation to stand by it. "Gotcha!" A backpack hit him on the head as he stood there, and he let his elbow jab into a stomach and felt glad when he heard a guttural "Oof!" Phil's knuckles were bone white as both hands clung onto the handrail. He turned slightly and saw that the doors were now fully open. He stood there, terrified, teeth clenched, jaw set and looked out onto a void.

There was nothing out there. No houses, no lights, nothing but darkness. Just the endless rain hitting his face and running down his neck. "No! No!" Hair in his eyes, the expensive shirt little more than a damp brightly coloured rag, he looked out into a black void. The train was still moving, and Phil closed his eyes. The phone vibrated in his pocket, but he ignored it. The train was picking up speed and he was surrounded. "You're not real!" he shouted "Let me off at the next stop! I won't say anything!"

There was a shove in the small of his back and he was pushed sharply against the carriage wall, hitting his head. The cold night air was making him shiver and then suddenly one of his hands lost its grip on the handrail and he was clinging on for dear life with the other one. Someone grabbed his free hand as it flailed and then tried to pull him towards the doors. "No, no please!" he shouted hating the tearful sound in his voice as his feet moved towards the open doors and his other hand began to lose its grip. He was being pulled and pushed until suddenly he was almost dangling over the open doorway. "No, no, no don't do this," he pleaded as he stood looking down into the void, his shirt flapping, the air icy on his stomach, his breathing was becoming harder. The vibration from his phone let him know that someone or something was there. "Stop pushing me whatever, whoever you are!" he shouted as the crowd behind became more determined. Phil's teeth were chattering as one hand clung determinedly to the handrail. Then he was teetering, his feet almost determined to walk over into the void. Phil's eyes began to roll up into his head and he was finding it difficult to breathe, he was so cold. "Got to hold on." But he was sinking, falling to the floor into unconsciousness. As he did so the doors closed, and the lights came on again carriage by carriage. The train sped on. Silence fell again and now the illuminated information board carriage indicator displayed that the all the carriages were empty, except for Phil's, which had only one occupant.

***

When he awoke, he was alone, lying on the floor.

"Ow!" he rubbed his aching ribs and a heel mark was beginning to appear on his hand. He lay on his back and stared up at the ceiling before slowly pulling himself into a sitting position. Automatically, he reached for his phone knowing that there would be more messages waiting for him.

Did you enjoy having company? Shame you had to bug out when we were all having fun. Angry face emoji.

"That isn't how I see it," Phil thought to himself.

Party pooper! Vexed face emoji.

"What do you want from me?" he tried to shout but could only manage a croak. A metallic rattle made him turn his head as he saw his discarded Red Bull can rolling down the carriage towards him.

Phil wondered if anyone was missing him. "The boys will be well away by now, on the pull, on the lash. They'll only miss me when they have to pay for their own Christmas dinner tonight. I'll never hear the end of it." He wondered how he'd fallen in with them. Safety in numbers was the way to get on in Swinson's. Play hard, work hard, although his frequent hangovers were beginning to be a problem. He'd caught himself pressing the wrong button on a spreadsheet and emailing it to a client once too often. The right clothes didn't come cheap either and he often felt alone even in the middle of them, red faced, tie loose, all looking at him to get the next round in. Again.

"Ow!" the Red Bull can hit him in the face, and he winced as he staggered back.

Spoilsport. Smiley face emoji.

"Stop it! I don't want to play anymore." Phil shouted as he ducked to avoid the crumpled can as it was aimed at him again. He quickly retreated back to the seats, crouching to the floor and rolling himself into a ball as it seemed to come at him from all angles. Eventually it stopped. Phil put his head up and noticed that light was coming in through the window.

"I can't have been on this bloody train all night!" he thought as he saw a pale pink sunrise beginning to illuminate the sky. "The rain's stopped. Streets, houses, lights – where are we?" He opened the window, picked up the can and threw it out before closing the window again.

But Max we're just getting acquainted. We're having such fun, aren't we? Smiley face emoji.

"I'm not Max. I'm Phil."

Didn't you get on at New Beckenham?" Phil suddenly remembered the pale face giving him the finger as the train moved off.

"Yes."

But you're not Max. Puzzled face emoji.

"No."

He had an appointment. Puzzled face emoji.

"He missed it then."

You weren't supposed to get on this train. Puzzled face emoji.

"Was the man at the station supposed to?"

Maybe. Smiley face emoji.

"But it wasn't supposed to stop there last night." The atmosphere on the train was changing, Phil felt his teeth go on edge. "Have you messed up?" he asked.

No, you did that when you got on instead of Max. Angry face emoji.

"What has Max done?"

None of your business. Angry face emoji.

Phil felt the urge to laugh at the absurdity of it all. But he felt that if he gave into it then he would never stop and soon it wouldn't be laughter anymore.

So, you're definitely not Max? You're not lying to me? Puzzled face emoji.

"No."

You won't remember any of this. Smiley face emoji

"I won't want to."

Good. But I'll need to make sure. Smiley face emoji.

Phil was suddenly scared. "You won't hurt me, will you?" he said as he looked anxiously down the empty train.

Too much paperwork for that. Smiley face emoji.

"Let me off at the next station. I won't say a word. Promise." Phil said.

They all say that. Smiley face emoji.

"Where are we going?" said Phil.

We have our own timetable. Smiley face emoji,

Phil looked around as he tried to stretch and then put his jacket on again.

"Show yourself, where are you?"

Why should I? The screen went blank.

The train was moving onto another line, clattering over a set of points. Phil watched as the brightly lit mainline receded behind overhanging trees and bushes. They jostled against the outside of the train, branches scratching and leaves swishing against it.

"Where are we going?" he shouted.

There are always odd lines, branch lines that don't appear on the maps. Smiley face emoji.

"A tunnel!" Phil shouted as he desperately looked out of the windows at darkness on either side. He hated tunnels and the train was going down, down, down into one. "Leave me alone! Let me out!" the heel mark on his hand was beginning to really hurt and when he touched it a trace of blood came away on his hand. He ran to the driver's door and banged on again. "Let me in! Please, please!" he pleaded. But, as he pulled on the door handle, it suddenly opened and he almost fell back. It stood ajar

Now, now, there's no need for all this fuss. Smiley face emoji. *You only had to ask.* Sad face emoji.

Phil stood and waited. The door continued to stand ajar. Sweat made Phil's face wet.

Aren't you going to come and say hello? Smiley face emoji.

The door opened further as if being pushed. Phil strode over and pulled the door open wide. The driver's cab was empty. Somehow, he had expected it. He looked through its window into the tunnel's darkness as the train sped on. He saw a movement behind him in the driver's window and quickly turned to prevent the door from closing on him by putting his foot out. Then he kicked it wide open again, entered the carriage again and then pushed the door back shut with a slam.

You're no fun. Sad face emoji.

"Neither are you." muttered Phil.

I suppose you'll have to do as we don't have Max. Smiley face emoji.

Phil turned around to face whatever was behind him. The Red Bull can bounced off his face as it came at him with force and he quickly turned his head. He shrank back as he smelt something primeval and animal like, hot breath and a stink of sulphur. It was almost touching him it was so close. Then the train was through the tunnel and slowing down as it entered the station. It stopped as Phil almost ran towards the doors. They opened and he threw himself through them and landed on the platform "Ow!" The phone fell from his pocket. The screen was illuminated.

You weren't supposed to get on this train, but you did. Don't do it again. Next time you might not be so lucky. Angry face emoji.

The dawn chorus was in full throttle as he lay there wondering where he was. The doors slammed shut behind him as the train moved off again, but as it did so, Phil thought that he saw a dark figure waving at him as it pulled out of the station.

Phil managed to get to his feet and then sat down on one of the metal seats on the platform to think about the night's events. "Who was Max? What did they want with him?" On the road above he could hear traffic, a red double decker bus trundled past and it was as if he'd never seen one before. Phil scrolled down the list of messages and videos from the gang.

Top night Phil what happened? Puzzled emoji from Dan.

Transport probs. He texted back and put the phone into his pocket. "This time I'll take the bus." He stood up and walked to the exit. It wouldn't take him long to pack, email his resignation and move on.

Meanwhile the train sat in the tunnel as a crumpled can of Red Bull ricocheted off the carriage walls and doors and ceiling over and over and over again. It waited. After all, it still had an appointment with Max.

JOY'S JOURNEY *MARGIT PHYSANT*

Joy was about to go out for the first time in a while, three years, two months and five days, to be precise. She had not been outside the house since that day, after which nothing was ever the same again. For protection, she dug out her father's Second World War service revolver and kept it in the hallway.

However, the day had arrived, and she was ready – albeit a bit apprehensive – to go out. Her therapist, Liz, had worked with her for months to build her confidence. The process of going out was divided into a series of tiny steps: put on shoes, put on shoes and overcoat, walk to the front door, unlock the door, open the door, stand in the doorway without going out. Each step was practiced until she felt a total sense of ease and could move on to the next stage.

When she first got to the "stand in the doorway" stage she noticed a man approaching on the pavement. He was some distance away, but she was enveloped by a fog of fear and had to rush back in. The process had to start all over again.

Anyway, she was now ready to take the first step outside. It went well, in fact she was able to walk several yards along the pavement before feeling the need to turn back. She continued to progress and could soon walk to the end of the street, even without Liz being present.

One day, as she was on her way back into her house, the phone rang. In the rush to answer it she left the door ajar, and did not hear the postman call out, 'Hello, is anyone there?' nor see him slowly push the door open.

When she finished her phone call and returned to the hallway, she saw the figure of a large man silhouetted against the door opening. Again, she felt the fog of fear close in on her, but managed to reach out for the gun on the hall shelf and take aim at the figure.

***

Dear Reader, this is where it can go several ways: we can always hope that fate intervenes. The revolver may not be loaded. And if it is, does it even work? It is, after all, an old weapon that has not been serviced for decades, so what are the chances? And what about the shooter, Joy, who has never fired a gun in her life? Will she be able to hit a target, let alone cause serious damage?

Alas, fate is not reliable. It can still go two ways. Those of us who value human life in general and postal workers in particular will favour the first version. What about Joy, the one with the finger on the trigger, at this moment the mistress of her own destiny? What is a good outcome for her?

***

Joy grabbed the gun, aimed it at the figure in the doorway and pulled the trigger. There was a loud bang and the man fell outwards onto the pavement.

She stood there, frozen, while he bled out. A passer-by called the emergency services, but he died on the way to the hospital. The victim turned out to be Pete, the local postman, doing his round.

She sank down into a foetal position where she stayed until the police came.

At the trial, the defence barrister pleaded self-defence on Joy's behalf and a psychiatrist testified that she had been diagnosed with post-traumatic stress disorder. Women's groups protested outside the courthouse. She was found guilty of manslaughter and received a ten-year prison sentence with the possibility of parole after five. After she was sentenced, a riot broke out in court.

Joy adjusted well to prison life. She enjoyed the predictability of the daily routine and felt comfortable within the confines of her cell. With no pressure to go outside and no men around she could relax, and felt happier than she had for a long time.

When she became eligible for parole, she did not apply.

***

Joy grabbed the gun, took aim at the figure in the doorway and was about to squeeze the trigger when the man called out, "Joy, it's me, Pete. Put that thing down, you scare me!"

She recognised him, and relaxed. Pete was the friendly postman who would ring the bell and ask if she wanted anything from the shops, and help with her small repairs. In return she would bake his favourite carrot cake and share it with him over a cup of tea. Joy always felt at ease in his company.

"I am so sorry, Pete, I didn't realise it was you."

"Don't worry, no harm done." Pete breathed a sigh of relief. "You sit down, I will make you a cup of tea."

They had tea together and when he had finished work, he called in – carefully shouting "It's only me," through the letterbox. Joy had calmed down and insisted he join her for supper. That suited Pete; he had nothing to go home for since his mother died, except an empty house and long evenings alone.

This became a regular occurrence. Pete stayed longer and longer until the day he did not go home anymore.

They were both very comfortable with this arrangement. Joy no longer had any desire to go outside, and discontinued her therapy. Liz tried to persuade her but eventually gave up. Joy never ventured outside again.

I'M GOING... *ANA CASTELLANI*

I'm going and I'm never to come back
You need not follow for I've made up my mind
It's my first time outside, but even though I'm scared
You need not follow, I'm never to come back

For years I've walked on your same path
My days have always been your own
But I'm outside of you and far from us
Don't follow me, I'm never to come back

My heart is screaming to get out and walk
My mind's made up, it doesn't need to change
I'm scared but if I start to walk
You need not follow, I'm never to come back

The ginger sun is beckoning to me
My eyes are filled with empty thoughts
My feet will carry me away from here
You need not follow, I'm never to come back

My path will take me out and that's enough
I'll steal your truck and I'll be out of here
I won't look back no matter what you shout
Don't dare to follow - I'm gone and you're my past.

ON THE LIST *DOMINIC GUGAS*

The alleyway was dead, and stank. Light and life and noise came from the doorway at the end of the alley, past the velvet rope and the hard-faced man guarding it. As far as Jason could see, or more to the point couldn't see, everything else was dark – the alley, the city, as far as he knew the entire world. The only signs of life were the endless line shuffling towards the club, and the odd furtive rustle among the garbage sacks that lined the sides.

The bouncer wasn't letting a lot of people in. Most, he turned away, and those he turned away vanished in a wash of warm yellow light. Jason didn't even feel curious about that. He knew that he ought to, that it wasn't something that usually happened, but it just felt right. Their names weren't on the list. They weren't getting in.

Some accepted meekly, and vanished straight away. Others tried pleading, or arguing, or slipping a bribe to the bouncer. The bribes he just refused, no matter how artfully offered and regardless of the size, with a shake of his head and a sneer as if to say he wasn't for sale to the likes of them, and the light would take them away, sometimes with the money still held in their outstretched hands. For those who pled or argued he just asked one question.

"What have you done?" Nobody's answer seemed to satisfy him, and so again the shake of the head and the sneer, and the light would claim them as well, and the line would shuffle forward. Again, and again, and again, until Jason found himself at the head of the line, where the bouncer looked at him, then down at his list.

"Jason Harvey?" he said, with a cold, hard smile. "You're on the list. You can go straight in."

"You lucky bastard," said the man behind Jason. "How come you get in?"

"Well, you know, I was quarterback for my college football team when we—"

"Oh, please," said the bouncer. "Nobody here has even heard of your college."

"Well then, could be because I'm the senior president for Asian commodities at—"

The bouncer cut him off again. "We have CEOs, celebrities and statesmen here every night. You're a small fish in this pond, mister."

"My charitable donations?"

"Really, nobody cares about your check book waving. Come on in, you're holding up the line."

With a shrug to the disgruntled individual behind him, Jason strode forward towards the club. As the bouncer lifted the velvet rope for Jason, he leaned over and whispered.

"You killed a child. Welcome to Hell."

MAY THE ROAD RISE *TIA FISHER*

May the road rise to meet you.
May the wind be always at your back.
May the sun shine warm upon your face.
May the rains fall soft upon your fields
And, until we meet again,
May God rest you in the palm of His hand.

— IRISH BLESSING (ANON)

W as the old man messing me about? Jesus, what a thing to ask me for. I stared back at him, at his face as grey and ruined as our old dishcloths. He blinked. I scratched my head.

He'd not be joking *now*, would he? Not inches away from his mortal end, with the oxygen tank hissing a warning and his eyes the colour of old piss?

No, I decided, he wouldn't. He'd asked me straight out, dead serious—no pun intended—not a flicker of a smile.

And because I knew it meant so much to him, and because I wanted to make him happy, I said, *Yes, of course, Dad, I'll do it for you, I will.* Even though I'd no idea of how I'd get it done.

***

That evening, we went to The Talbot Arms to talk it over. Dad's three sons: Ethan, Rory, and me. We went to the pub because it didn't seem right to talk about his dead body within earshot of his living self in that hospital bed we'd set up downstairs, so we called in the nurse to sit with him.

I was having a hard job persuading Ethan it was workable. "Go on, he just wants a sort of wake," I said. "We've got no wheelchair, but we could—I don't know—put him in a Tesco trolley or something." There was no way we'd shift that iron monster of a bed up the hill, wheels or no wheels, not even with three of us pushing.

"Yeah, that's right, they do wakes all the time back home." Rory nodded as if he knew what he was talking about and set his empty glass down with a clunk. Seemed like that last whiskey had settled the argument.

Ethan wasn't having it, though. "Not like this, and not with the body in a feckin' shopping trolley, they don't!" He slapped his tobacco pouch onto the table and started rolling, little shreds of baccy going everywhere. "And anyway, no-one does wakes in England."

I thought of Dad. How he'd smiled and sank back into sleep after we said we'd do it. "Weren't you there with me back then, promising him we'd carry out his last wish? Did you have your fingers crossed behind your back then, is that it?"

Ethan's ears went red with frustration, but he knew what he'd said. He retreated out the back for a sulk and a smoke.

Considering I'd just bought six rounds of beer with whiskey chasers, I judged now to be a good moment to ask Pete behind the bar if it would be okay with him. I reckoned that if I could get one of the pubs on board, the others would agree, for fear of looking bad.

Pete stopped tapping at his phone for a second and looked kind of surprised, but then he said he'd a lot of feeling for my dad, he'd been a good customer, the sort that always says sorry afterwards. He said he'd have a think about it, and I should come back tomorrow.

So, the next day, there I was, banging on the door at opening time to ask Pete if he'd made up his mind. I wasn't wanting to be pushy, but there was no time to lose, with Dad looking more like a waxwork every day, and the family back home Whats-

Apping on the hour to ask when we thought the funeral would be because Ryanair tickets were going up every day, and they didn't know what they'd do if he lasted till Christmas.

Dad was Irish, of course. I don't know why I say *of course*, except maybe it explains why he wanted this last, post-mortem, pub crawl all the way up the steepest hill of our steep-hilled seaside town. Dad wanted us to wheel him in for a last stop at the five hostelries which were spaced out along its mile-long gasp-fest. *The Stations of the Cross*, Dad called them. Before he got so sick, he'd drop in to each in turn for *just a refresher* on his way home from work at the harbour. Every weeknight for thirty years, fuelling himself for the long climb up to our home at the crest of the hill.

Ours wasn't like the other posh houses on the summit. It wasn't an old-English-money mansion with crenelated walls and acres of garden and keep-the-fuck-off-my-land signs to stop the tourists from straying in. Ours was a shabby little bungalow, too small for a widower and his three grown-up sons who'd not moved on with their lives; a flimsy sixties build somehow smuggled in when no-one in the planning department was looking. Servants' quarters. If tourists had appeared in our wind-filled, junk-strewn yard, Dad would have shaken them warmly by the hand and asked them in for a coffee, *mind the wobbly step, won't you now?* That was the kind of man he was. Had been. Was.

Pete said no. Of course he did, the bastard. *Health and safety, health and safety*, he kept saying. *Can't be done. Risk of infection.* I told him that Dad had spent twenty years coughing, sneezing, farting and occasionally puking in this pub, and—quite apart from the loyalty angle—they'd already had all the germs that his corpse was likely to pass on. He had liver cancer, for Christ's sake, not the fucking plague. Then Pete pulled out his trump card and said he'd spoken to the brewery and *they'd* said no, and then it was like he'd bought back the word of Moses, there was no shifting him. To give him credit, he did look sorry about it, but so he should, all the Friday-night wage packets my dad had emptied in his place.

There didn't seem much point in asking in the other pubs: they were all owned by the same brewery except for the one free house, The Old Black Dog, and Dad still had a big tab owing there, so I went back to tell my brothers that our plan was dead in the water.

No matter that he'd been so against the idea less than twenty-four hours ago, Ethan was outraged. "They can't deny a man his dying wish!" He banged the wall beside him, making it shake. "Bunch o' feckin' wankers! I'll put it on Trip Advisor, they'll be sorry."

Rory looked really upset. He trailed into the front room, where our Dad was sleeping like he mostly did these days. "I'm sorry, Da," I heard him whisper.

But I think I felt the worst, because I was the oldest, and it was all down to me to take care of everything: take care of our father, take care of Rory, and now take care of this, this last *fart* of a wish from our gentle, joking, drunken Dad.

I thought of maybe getting together a petition among the regulars, because Dad was well-liked—but there really wasn't time for that, and anyway, since when did the breweries give a toss?

I joined Rory in the front room, and bent down to give our father a kiss on his forehead. Something about his skin felt wrong against my lips. "Dad? *Dad*?"

Ethan must have heard the panic in my voice because he came rushing in, and we stood in silence, holding hands like we hadn't done since we were kiddies, watching that scrawny yellow chest for a breath that didn't come.

Rory was the first to stop crying. He laid Dad's chicken-claw hand back on the covers and raised his sad wet face to me.

"I don't care what Pete said! We're doing it. We're doing it!"

"It can't be done. The pubs won't let us." Ethan's voice was bitter.

But Rory pleaded. "Please, please, *please*. Dad wanted it. We promised."

And we looked at him lying there, the *Da* who had bathed us and sung to us and bought us our first pints, and I knew that we needed to do this for him, not to let him down. It might be the most idiotic thing I'd ever heard of, but it was what he'd wanted, and we loved him.

I wiped my eyes. "We're doing it. But it's got to be quick—before anyone finds out he's passed." And before he stiffens up, I thought, but there was no need to say that. "We're to go out as soon as it gets dark." I told Rory and Ethan to get Dad dressed in his best—and only—suit, while I went to the supermarket for the rest of what was needed. I had a plan.

The cancer had shrunk Dad's limbs to sticks: his funeral suit looked almost empty, so just like we did when we were kids, we stuffed the arms and legs of our 'guy' with socks, and tied them at the wrist and ankle to keep it all tight.

I admit, I did hesitate before putting the Boris mask over his face, but this late on Bonfire Night it was all they'd had left.

Ethan urged me on. "Nah, Dad'd get the joke, sure he would. He'd be feckin' pissing himself!"

So I did, I put it on, and when it was finished, we stepped back to look. Honestly, all done up in the wig, mask and rubber gloves, you couldn't tell the figure in the trolley had ever breathed.

It was Rory who came up with the finishing touch. He cut the side off a cardboard box and wrote in thick, black, wobbly, letters:

PENNY FOR THE GUY!
PLEASE GIVE GENRUSLY!
FIGHT LIVER CANCER!!!

I didn't tell him about the spelling. Dad always said that Rory's heart was bigger than his brain, and it was true enough.

I found some old Irish Tricolour bunting that Dad had got in for the rugby and gussied up the trolley with it, and then we were ready. There was a little struggle to get him up over the step, but we were out of the door by five-fifteen. In the deserted street it was drizzling a damp, grey, miserable mist, so as an afterthought, I popped back into the house and balanced Dad's trilby on top of Boris's blonde mop.

Ethan wanted to start at the top of the hill, but I said no, we had to go all the way to the bottom first and work our way upwards, because that's the way Dad always did it. First, he'd have a pint of gat at The Volunteer Inn, then another in The Nag's Head. Ever since they'd tarted up The Mariner's Hotel, Dad didn't feel welcome, so usually he just had a quick piss there before he went on to The Talbot Arms. He'd always finish the night by having a pint and a fight with the barman at The Old Black Dog.

As we set off downhill, the first fireworks started to pop and fizzle. Brightness flared briefly against the dusk.

The plan was to go into every pub, raise a glass of the black stuff to our darling Da, throw it quickly down the open gullets we'd inherited from him, and push on to the next. So early in the evening as it was, the pubs would be pretty empty: a few out-of-season day-trippers, a sprinkling of regulars. We should be home by eight thirty: we'd get Dad back into bed, and then we'd call the MacMillan, like it said on the leaflet. No-one would be any the wiser, and Dad would have visited his Stations of the Cross one last time.

But it didn't happen exactly that way.

For starters, did I mention it was a one-in-eight hill? Even though our Dad was down to the bones, once we'd picked up momentum, it was hard work hanging on to that trolley. I was the brakeman at the back while Ethan and Rory held the sides, almost running beside our Dad, who obviously had a heck of a thirst on him. A few times I thought we were going to lose our grip, and Dad was going to hurtle down the hill, all the way to the bottom and straight over the harbour wall. Not that he would have minded a burial at sea, but it would have caused us a lot of problems.

It got worse when the trolley developed a wonky wheel and we started to slalom, so in the end, Rory walked in front to hold us straight, with Dad's best brogues pressing into the small of his back, and then it was kind of a procession, like a proper funeral thing.

Trouble was, I'd not realised what a stir three grown men pushing Boris Johnson in a flag-draped shopping trolley would make. Even on Bonfire Night, eyebrows were raised.

We tried to ignore the looks from passers-by, but just as we were starting the journey up the hill again, Mrs Huggins from the launderette appeared, handbag swinging like a wrecking ball. She blocked our progress and leaned forward in the gloom to take a good long look at our father's corpse, her orange-lipsticked mouth pursed into a cat's arse of disapproval.

"What's this, then?" she asked, and peered at the sign Rory had written.

I noticed a tuft of dark hair escaping from under the wig and was struck mute, but luckily, she didn't pause for long. She never did.

"So that's what your father's got, is it? Liver cancer?" she continued, nodding at Ethan.

He nodded back miserably.

"Then he won't be spending this in the pub, at least," she said, "I'll see if I've got any change." While she rummaged in the bottom of that huge handbag, I quickly tugged Dad's wig back into place.

"Here you are," she said, and looked around for somewhere to put her fifty pee.

Quick as anything, Rory snatched the hat off Dad's head and held it out to her. Ethan and I exchanged looks. That boy had all the right instincts.

Mrs Huggins lingered, wanting to share her views on street charity collectors, but Ethan shouldered his way between her and the trolley before she could really gather pace. "Thank you kindly, Mrs H. But we'll have to be getting on now."

"Oh. Well, pass my best to your father, Ethan. And remember, hope never dies."

Ethan nodded, straight-faced. "Indeed, it doesn't, Mrs Huggins, indeed it doesn't. Come on, Rory!" He grabbed the hat from our brother and rested it in the valley of Dad's crotch.

From then on, it seemed like every soul who saw us sweating and struggling to keep our laden trolley on an even keel, sighed at our fortitude and charity, and dug deep in their pockets to spare us some change.

Inside The Volunteer, we pushed Dad into a dark corner and avoided eye contact with the other patrons, but there was no stopping their generosity. Like sheep at a salt lick, they crowded around him and threw in their coins, one after the other. I admit it was wrong—it was deeply wrong on all kinds of levels—but what could we do? We drank up as quickly as we could and left, but still, the hat was full by the time we reached the second station of the cross.

We stopped in the lee of The Nag's Head's brick-built porch.

Rory rested up against the trolley while Ethan counted the cash. A total of twenty-seven pounds and forty pee.

"Jesus," said Rory, his mouth a round O of wonder. "And we wasn't even trying!"

"Weren't." I murmured automatically. "Weren't even trying."

"Bog off, bookworm!" Rory jabbed two fingers up at me. 'Bookworm' was his favourite insult for his oldest brother because I wrote books: not the most inspired put-down.

Ethan stared at the money, the odd fiver sticking up between the coins. "What're we supposed to do with this, then?" He held the hat away from his body like it was full of dog shit.

But the way I saw it, we had two options. Either we actually gave it to charity, or—

"We should do what Dad would have done, of course," I said, and turned my back on the street to scoop the cash into my coat pockets. With any luck, we might get enough to pay off his bill at The Dog.

The Old Black Dog was certainly old. Crumbling even. It offered its patrons both the best beer and the worst service in town, and by the time we'd pushed Dad up to his last watering hole, we were ready for that beer. All three of us were panting like the pub mascot, a three-foot-high plaster Doberman which stood on guard beside the narrow entrance.

An entrance so narrow that we couldn't get the trolley through. We tried pushing, then pulling from the other side, but Dad just got wedged into the rotting architrave and we had to give up. With disabled access we'd have been fine, but The Dog wasn't one to mollycoddle its patrons.

"Ah, frigging *feck*!" wheezed Ethan, and spat a huge grey glob of smokers' phlegm at the dog's paws. He pulled out his pouch to roll up. "What'll we do now? We can't leave Dad outside on the street."

"And we can't *not* go in, neither. We promised him—every Station," said Rory, his sweaty forehead all creased.

"Hold on, let's just get our breath back while I count this. I'll have a think."

I added up the latest coins and handed them to Ethan because my pockets could hold no more. I was keeping a tally in my head. Minus the money for drinks to toast him with—and we'd had no chasers, mark you, out of respect and the need for haste—we had fifty-eight pounds and sixty-two pee left.

"Who puts *two pee* in a bucket?" said Ethan, holding up the copper between two nicotined fingers. "Cheap fecker."

The door opened from inside, and Alan the barman poked his greasy head out. "I heard you lot was coming," he said sourly. "Quite the fuss you've been making, all the way up the hill. So are you going to stand there all day and block my trade?"

I pointed to the trolley, by which Ethan was now standing, smoking his fag, Dad's head resting comfortably against his thigh. "We can't come in, can we? Can't get this in. Your doorway's too small."

"And your trolley's too big. Why not just leave it outside?"

asked Alan.

Since we couldn't think of a reason why not—or not one that we could let on—we ended up using the Doberman as a chock to stop Dad rolling backwards, and filed inside to drink to his health. His sort-of health.

As I'd known he would, Alan rummaged inside the till and handed over a grubby slip of paper with Dad's tab scribbled on it. I scowled at him, but paid the tab, and we drank the balance as quickly as we could, not wanting to leave Dad alone outside on his own for too long. Then we all went for a piss.

"Done it. We *done* it!" Beside me, Ethan swayed and leaned his head against the cool tiles. "We done him proud, we have."

"He'd've loved the craic, for sure," said Rory, zipping up. "Shame about havin' to leave him outside here, though. D'you think he minded?"

I thought about it. I belched up a rich taste of Guinness. "Hard to tell, in the mask."

We headed out of the Gents.

Where the trolley had been, was only blank space. I turned my head frantically from side to side as though Dad might be playing hide-and-seek nearby, praying it wasn't true. But it was: the trolley had gone. Vanished. The long-tongued Doberman was still there, lying on his side in the grass, but no sign of the trolley. Some fucking guard dog he was.

"*DA!!!!!!*" shouted Rory. "Where *are* you?" He peered behind the hedge like our dead father had just wandered off for a wee slash.

"Shut up, you ejit!" Ethan hissed. "Look, he can't've gone off by himself, can he?"

I held out an arm. "Shhhhhh!"

And we all shushed and listened, and sure enough, between the cracks of fireworks, we could hear it, that *eek-eeek-eek-eeek-eek* of the wonky wheel.

"This way!" Ethan pointed right, up the hill, and off we set off in pursuit.

I felt like I was doing the Tour de France, only with no bicycle and seven pints of heavy in my gut. After the first fifty metres I thought I'd likely die, and beside me I could hear Ethan's lungs hating him. But young Rory was racing ahead, his big thighs pumping, his boots thudding onto the pavement. He'd been the One Hundred Metres Country Champion until the hormones kicked in.

I narrowed my eyes through the sweat trickling in them, to peer ahead. It was dark at this end of the road; too dark to make much out until we got to the top of the hill, but then the firework display in the park reached its finale in a torrent of noise and light. A crescendo of flashes lit up the small group of lads clustered around our trolley like they were in no-man's land.

"You thievin' feckin' *gits!*" yelled Ethan and adrenaline kicked him up the arse: he turbo-charged up the slope towards them, waving his tobacco pouch like a tomahawk.

They looked around, startled.

Ethan burst in, scattering the boys like a pool break. "*Leave him alone!*" he screamed, and they trickled back down the hill, swearing loudly to each other.

All except one, who stayed where he was, a hand resting heavily on Dad's shoulder. The rockets bursting overhead showed me a pasty face and a defiant chin decorated by a pubic tuft of boy-beard. Lion logos stitched onto his baseball cap and bomber jacket told me all I needed to know. My hackles rose.

"Get your hands off our da—*dummy!* Get—get ..." But then a stitch chewed at my ribs and I collapsed into coughing. Still, what I lacked in gravitas, I made up for in bulk. I was about four stone heavier than Pastyface: I didn't need to sound impressive as well.

But this boy wasn't about to back down, even against such overwhelming odds. "What's the big deal?" He looked at Dad's body and his hand edged towards the mask.

"Don't feckin' *touch* him!" warned Ethan, moving forward.

"Why not?" The lad tweaked Boris's nose between thumb

and forefinger. I saw puzzlement flash across his face as he must have felt flesh and bone through the latex. He reached to rip the mask off—

"*NO!*" Rory bellowed, and leapt forward. He gave the trolley an almighty push away from the lad, sending it careering off the pavement and onto the road. Luckily, it didn't tip over, but gravity snatched the wheels and we watched our father's corpse rattling down the pot-holed road, head bobbing, arms and legs jiggling wildly. I took a millisecond to curse my father's dying wish, then ran like fuck after him.

"Are you alright?" asked Rory, poking Dad gingerly.

"He's fine," I said, panting. It was me that wasn't.

Our cadaver's bid for freedom had been mercifully short: a long level stretch outside The Talbot had slowed him down enough for us to catch hold. Miraculously, he'd not fallen out: the mask and wig were intact, and he was only missing his trilby. A shock of white blonde hair glinted brightly under The Talbot's lit pub sign. Through the medium of Boris Johnson, our dead-sober Dad stared up at us smugly, like this had been his plan all along.

Holding tight onto the trolley, we laboured up the hill again to home. It seemed to take a very long time.

On the front step, I was having trouble finding the key. Actually, I was having trouble finding my pocket.

"Will you not hurry with that door?" Ethan was gasping still, gripping Dad's shoulder for support. Sweat shone from his face. "I don't feel so good."

Neither did I. The horizon wouldn't stay still, and now I had it, the bastard key wouldn't fit in the lock. I gave it up and rounded off the night by heaving behind the bins, just like my daddy would have done.

***

His voice was thin through the hiss of oxygen, but I could understand him.

"Oh ... oh, that's good ... that's good ... that's funny... what'll you call it?"

"I dunno.... *Off his Trolley*, maybe?"

It was a faint chuckle, but Dad was laughing, definitely laughing. The mask wobbled up and down over the bridge of his beaky nose. "Ah ... you've done me ... proud. At last, a story of me own ... all about me."

"Yeah. Sorry it was only a short story, but—"

"I know. No time."

He coughed and I helped him spit into the bowl, then lowered him back down against the pillows as gently as I could. I pulled the covers up over ribs which looked like park railings.

"It will help ... you know ... writing. Writing about me, about…. Help you to…." Dad trailed off and his eyes closed, exhausted with the effort of speaking.

I watched him slip into morphine dreams, then stood up and tucked the manuscript under his thin hand.

"Just for you, Da," I said. "May the road rise to meet you."

PASSAGE *ALISON BENNETT*

Past midnight, the road empty,
streaked with salt, a crust of ice,
I see reflection.
Fox eyes bright beside a hedge
then gone.

I pass through winter trees,
bare common, frozen sky,
radio not quite drowning
the incessant
might-have-beens
could-have-beens
nevers.

TRAVELLERS' TALES *HC JOHNSTON*

Tony and Mike were hiking in the country. The morning was bright, the road was level. Land undulated around them like a calm ocean, uninterrupted. In the distance, blue hills faded towards the violet line of the horizon. Fields succeeded woodland along the roadside, and forests only loomed at a safe distance.

They were unencumbered by electronics: they had agreed to leave their iPods, Fitbits, and smart watches behind, and their mobiles were only to be used for really dire emergency, like attack by a pack of wolves. Certainly not for something as ordinary as a GPS reading, or a map.

"Why do we need a map?" said Tony. "The road's so straight you could put a ruler down it, and we know where it goes and how far."

Mike had burbled a little, so they agreed to take the mobiles but not to switch them on. Tony had wanted to leave them behind altogether, but Mike muttered about the kind of horror film when strangers get lost in the woods and end up trapped in a cabin by a wild-haired guy with an unfocussed blue stare. And a chainsaw.

"Captain Cook managed without," said Tony.

"And if you could navigate by the stars, so could you," said Mike. "You can't find your way round the Tube map."

Compromise agreed.

Little breezes played around them; the summer air was warm but not stifling. They could smell a buoyancy, as if Nature herself was walking beside them, laying out green growth in their way, encouraging them on.

"I wish I knew what the trees were called," said Mike.

"Why? You can call them what you like, they don't care. I shall call that one Hubert." Tony pointed at a large oak.

"Not what I meant. I mean, I feel kind of ignorant, like there's a whole city out there all happening and I can't really see any of it."

"I've brought a field guide," said Tony. "A book. Look it up in that."

So, for a few moments, Mike did. "Beech," he said. "I think. Maybe."

There were no motor vehicles on the road, and nor should there be; this was a track for walkers and cyclists only. The surface was dry dirt, with a shallow ditch to mark the edges. No other walkers were in sight, and the gravel was too rough to show footprints of man or beast.

"It's probably too early," said Mike. "Not many people set out before breakfast."

"Is that a hint?" said Tony.

They stopped, sat on a boulder beside the road, and ate their date and macadamia energy bars. The sunlight was warm on their hair.

"UV?" said Mike.

"Not yet," said Tony. "Middle of the day. I've brought the slop, you won't die of cancer. Sunglasses, maybe." Tony, of course, had Raybans, which looked cool and upmarket, like Steve McQueen on the French Riviera. Mike had an anonymous pair from some supermarket.

"What's odd," said Mike, "is that I can't see any junctions on this road. There must be places where paths cross over it."

"Optical illusion," said Tony. "Heat haze." They set off again.

A sound. Faint, but insistent, a hum, a buzz. Behind them. Mike turned and saw a little buggy approaching, the sort that elderly people use on side-roads, covered with a soft plastic roof and windshield but open at the side. The buggy was black, with a walking stick in the back, and the driver was a bald man, possibly in his eighties. He waved as he approved.

"Nice day for it."

"Very nice," said Mike. "Where are you off to?"

"I'm meeting a friend – well, a contact. Sorry I can't give you a lift!"

"That's very kind," said Tony. "But we're out here on a bit of an adventure."

"Aren't you all?" said the man. "Well, can't delay. Bye for now." He waved, and the buggy whizzed into the distance.

Mike was working his way through the field guide, and could now, without too much hesitation, identify oak, beech, birch and brambles. The fuzzy green stuff that wasn't a tree was taking longer.

"Maybe it's a bluebell."

"Shouldn't they be blue?"

Apparently, and confusingly, the answer to that was 'not always' but Mike decided not to expose the issue, as it would lead to an argument neither could solve. Tony picked a piece of long grass from the roadside, and chewed it.

A bell rang behind them – then more than one.

"Bloody cyclists," said Mike. "Think they own the bloody road. Okay, who's doing the Tour de Home Counties?"

But when they turned, the three cyclists were not lycra-clad racers, but old ladies on distinctly old-fashioned machines. And they were wearing skirts.

"My gran used to ride a bike like that," said Tony. "They weigh an absolute ton. They must have thighs like Chris Hoy under that tweed."

The ladies approached them in a V formation, and slowed for a chat.

"Nice day for it," said the first. She had a pannier on her bike, a woven basket last seen, as far as Mike was concerned, in an episode of 'Miss Marple'.

"Very nice," said Mike. "Going somewhere interesting?"

"Knitting circle," said the second. "We go twice a week."

"Well, the goats never stop growing the wool, so we have to keep spinning it," said the third. "It would be a shame just to waste it."

"Look," said the first, and held up a neatly spun hank of white wool from her pannier. "That would cost you a fortune in London."

"We keep thinking about alpacas," said the third. "They're very amenable animals."

"But not classic," said the second. "And they're ruddy expensive."

"I'm more for cashmere," said the first. "I quite fancy a cashmere shawl."

"Tomorrow's decision," said the third, and they laughed.

"Bye for now," they said, and rode away towards the horizon.

"Knitting, on a day like today," said Tony. "Just the idea makes me hot and itchy."

The roadside changed from fields to light woodland, giving some grateful shade from the sun, and once more they stopped and sat down, and drank some water from their bottles. In the quiet, a robin hopped about in the dusty road, and a blackbird chortled above their heads.

"Hazel," said Mike. "This is a hazel coppice. They cut the branches to make fences and baskets."

"Well, aren't you the country type," said Tony.

"This is nice." Mike lay back on the plants under the bushes – dog's mercury and cow parsley. He dozed, for a couple of minutes. Tony fidgetted.

"Must press on," said Tony.

So they did.

About half an hour later, they heard a faint rhythmic crunching noise – and once more, they were no longer alone on the road.

This time, it was a walker. But a walker with a capital W, not a rambler or wanderer or stroller: the tall, spare man was dressed in serious fitness gear, the latest multi-coloured trainers on his feet. He was walking intensely as if he were skiing, using two sticks, each of which came up to his shoulders.

"Morning," said Mike, as the man approached.

The man looked up, as if interrupted, and frowned: an unfriendly expression. He grunted.

"I've seen those," said Tony. "Nordic walking poles, aren't they?"

"Some say so." The man did not stop walking, so they sped up slightly to keep pace. He had a slight foreign accent.

"This must be a good road for speed walking," said Mike.

"Yes, is good," the man said, but did not take his eyes off the road ahead, apart from glancing at his electronic tracker on a wristband.

"Strava, is that?" said Tony. "I've been told I should get one."

"For serious walker, yes," said the man. His tone had the hint of a sneer – or maybe it was just his accent.

Now Mike noticed that the man's tee-shirt had an inscription on the back: 'Thirty Thousand K Challenge' and beneath that, 'Kapitein H. Van der Drecken, Team Nederlands'.

"Are you Captain Drecken?"

The man stopped and glared at Mike. "Kapitein VAN DER Drecken, if you please. Now, I am ten seconds behind! This is intolerable! I must make up time!" He put an extra ten centimetres into his stride, and swore.

They let him walk ahead.

"Bastard," said Tony. "We were just being sociable."

"We're not serious walkers," said Mike. "Not serious to death, anyway. Look. A red kite."

"Oh, yes," said Tony, without looking up.

And an hour later, they heard the familiar, approaching buzz of wheeled bike on raw road behind them.

"Do you know," said Tony, "I picked this route because it was supposed to be quiet? It's like ruddy Piccadilly Circus."

"Lots of people like quiet," said Mike. "That's the quintessential contradiction of life today."

The bicycles drew closer: three of them, modern in design, ridden by athletic women in their late thirties in helmets, lycra and spiked shoes. But the clothes were muted in colour and designed for use, not show: keen club riders, maybe.

"Hi," said the first. "Have you seen anyone ahead of you?"

"Loads," said Tony. "Who are you looking for?"

"Our uncle," said the second. "He's in a mobility thingy."

"He'll have got himself in a fix,' said the third. "Honestly, he knows he should wait for us."

"Oh, you know him," said the second. "He's not very good with rules. Well, as long as we can catch up. When did he go past?"

"About an hour and a half ago," said Mike.

"Oh, flip," said the first. "We'd better put a wiggle on, then. Ta!" And she and her friends mounted their bicycles, took up a racing position and pedalled furiously into the distance, in a cloud of dust.

"Peace at last," said Tony.

But not quite. A few moments later, Mike's eye was caught by a movement in the bushes beside the road. After a few seconds, a man came out and beckoned to them. He looked terrified.

"Are they all gone?" he said.

They looked up and down the empty road.

"Yep, just us chickens," said Mike.

"Can we help you?" said Tony.

"Are they gone? Really?" said the man. He was mid-height, slightly built, and sallow-faced, wearing a down-at-heel suit with a fine dusting of soil.

"Really," said Mike. "Look, we've got our mobiles with us – do you want us to call someone?"

The man shook his head. "THEY might be listening," he said. "Has HE gone past?"

"Who he?"

"The—" The man swallowed. "The old one."

"Ages ago," said Tony. "He said he was going to a meeting."

The man twitched, and licked his lips. "Good. That's good. I must—" And then he ran back into the bushes.

"Blimey," said Tony, "they're all out today. It must be National Saint Nutter's Day."

But not more than ten minutes later, they saw a small blot on the road approaching them. The buggy had reappeared, and the driver was not a happy man.

"Bastard!" he cried out. "Not blasted well there! Bastard tried to pull the wool over! He owes me! Have you seen him?"

"We're not sure," said Tony."

"Your nieces came past," said Mike. "They seemed worried about you."

"Oh, them," said the man. "Never there when they're useful. Ha! Now I'm late for the next one!"

And he did what was presumably the closest the buggy could get to a handbrake turn, and zipped off down the road again, gesticulating.

Frankly, it was no great surprise when, twenty minutes later, Mike and Tony came across what could only be described as a pile-up. The buggy was on its side and the driver was perched on a fallen tree-trunk, catching his breath and being patted on the back by one of the Lycra cyclists. Van Der Drecken was sitting on the roadside, looking shocked, his walking poles scattered. And the other two women in Lycra were talking to the ladies in tweed, who seemed to have stopped for a roadside picnic – a tablecloth was laid out on the grass with plastic boxes and thermos flasks.

"Well, he came out of nowhere," said one lady. "Honestly, nobody could have stopped in time."

"Unavoidable," said the second lady. "No room to get past."

"Cut off in his prime," said the third. "Cruel, but it happens."

And then Mike and Tony spotted the poor, crumpled remains of the man in the suit at the roadside. He seemed empty, like a rag doll: there was no blood, just a carelessly thrown-down set of limbs and a skinny body half-twisted.

"Dear God, is he dead?" said Mike.

"Bastard," said the old man. "I'd told him where I was meeting him! I told him! Why'd he have to mess things up!"

"It's all right, Uncle," said the woman in Lycra."

"Not my time,' said Van Der Drecken. "Just – not my time, eh?" He muttered as if to himself and checked his Strava again. "Not my time. Not this time." He struggled to his feet.

"For God's sake, man, give yourself a breather?" said Mike. "Anyway, the police might want to speak to you."

And that really scared Van Der Drecken. "Police? No, not that, not again, not that, I have been judged, I have been condemned, I serve my time! I serve my time!" He was shouting.

"Concussion," said one of the other Lycra cyclists. "Here, sit down, Hendrik. You must wait. You know how this works. No matter how long it takes. No exceptions."

"What about the body?" said Tony, in a small voice.

"I told him where I was meeting him!" The old man would not keep still.

"Well, you met him anyway," said the knitter with the pannier. "Just not the way he thought."

The Lycra cyclist came over to Mike and Tony. "No need for you to hang around. We're contacted everyone who needs to know and you didn't see anything, did you? Just give us your numbers."

So Mike and Tony gave her their mobile numbers, and walked down the road once more. After a while, they could not hear the chatter at the accident site.

They said nothing for an hour, the shock of death taking the wind out of both of them, but eventually the spring came back to their step, they focussed on the journey again and the day bloomed around them. At least it did for Mike. As they walked on, they passed a grove of nettles and its accompanying cloud of Red Admiral butterflies.

"Why Admiral?" said Tony. "Admirals don't wear red, do they?"

"Used to be the Red Admirable," said Mike. "I prefer the Latin name. Vanessa atalantae. That means Atalanta's nymph or spirit. They're a symbol of the soul, in a lot of stories."

"Are they?" said Tony.

"Um, can I ask something? Not to be dreary or anything, but are we nearly there yet?"

"Must be," said Tony.

The day was fading a little now, the sun not as high, not as blazing, but the violet horizon seemed no closer. They walked on in companionable silence, keeping pace with their energy, neither speeding up nor slowing down, and on either side, field succeeded woodland succeeded grass or reeds. Where there was water, the swifts and martins screamed through the air, chasing mosquitoes; where it was dry, butterflies flickered and bees thundered from flower to flower. Once, Mike thought he spotted a roebuck, but it sauntered back into the woodland shade, utterly unperturbed.

Then Tony said, "You know, I think I'll just sit down for a moment. There's plenty of time. You go on, I'll catch you up."

"Are you sure? Will you know the way?"

Tony laughed. "That's easy, what's the saying? 'Second to the right, and straight on till morning.' I'm hardly going to get lost, am I."

Which was true.

The sky became a deeper blue, and a faint golden tinge lit the trees and hills, then gleamed stronger. Mike walked on. The first bats appeared – pipistrelles, probably, he was not close enough to pick out their features. The scents of the hedgerow changed, as night began to take over the little kingdoms by the roadside. Starlings went over in a rush, in a perfectly random cloud of mathematical form, squealing and chattering. And still he walked, on his own but never alone.

The path before him seemed to glow in the last of the sun, or perhaps the first moonbeams. There was no reason to stop, anyway. He was not tired, or afraid, or lost. In the deep sapphire of the evening, the diamond brilliance of Venus now shone over his way.

"Just follow that star," he said to himself. "Keep an eye out. Second to the right, then straight on till morning."

So he did that.

A THOUSAND KISSES DEEP *RAYMOND LITTLE*

Cohen had been dead almost two years when we came to the island.

Maisie spotted it first, and nudged my elbow. "Jack, look." I glanced up from the newspaper on my lap and saw it rising from the Aegean against a sky that still held the blueness of summer as if unaware that autumn had begun. We had bench seats in the bow of the ferry and spent the short journey from the mainland smoking and doing the crossword.

"This is it, then," I said. Whitewashed houses rose from the front before scattering into the hills, and I wondered if one of these might be Cohen's place. I draped an arm over Maisie's bare shoulders and felt her lean into me. The combination of us sitting in the shade of the front cabin and the breeze coming off the sea took any warmth from our skin and I felt goose-bumps under my palm.

"Come on." Maisie took my hand and we walked to the front rail, back into the early evening sunlight. Others had gathered there, taking pictures with their phones. I didn't bother, for the same reason I don't photograph concerts, landmarks, cats or, God forbid, my breakfast; you miss the moment. The boat let out a honk and slowed, and we were soon on the boardwalk with our luggage. We had booked a place close to the ferry port as we knew cars were not allowed on the small island, and approached an old man on a bench who was speaking Greek to the dog sitting between his feet.

"Hello," I said. He squinted at me, then Maisie, who he reserved a smile for. "Do you know this address, by any chance?" I handed him a slip of paper.

He nodded, and pointed a gnarled, brown finger. "This road. Halfway. Yes? See flag?"

I gazed in the direction he indicated and saw a flash of blue and white on a flagpole less than two hundred yards away. "I see it. Thanks."

"First time?"

"Yes."

"This is most special of all the islands." He waved his arm in a wide arc as if gifting us all we could see.

"It looks amazing," Maisie said. "Are you from here?"

"Live here all my life. No other place like it. You will see."

It took less than five minutes to reach the little hotel where a teenage boy emerged from the foyer to help with our bags and Maisie's easel. I tipped and thanked him, and he flashed a smile of white interrupted by one gold incisor. "Welcome to Hydra."

***

It was late after we unpacked so we decided to leave the trip to Cohen's house until the morning in favour of food. The sky was a deep lavender, and we walked along the narrow sea-front promenade where yellow light shone from tavernas and bars onto outside seating where healthy-looking locals and tourists had begun to enjoy the promise of night-time. This had been my favourite time of day since childhood, when the atmosphere would inch its way through shades of blue and purple to the eventuality of darkness, bringing with it a hush as the birds settled in their nests.

We found a little place up a side street which had an empty table for two on the pavement, and shared a seafood dish that came served on a plank of wood. The taverna was filled with quiet talk and laughter, and I looked along the alley at the bay where the reflected light from moored boats shimmered on the water's surface. It felt like the kind of place we could be happy. I sipped my wine and looked at Maisie, her face up-lit by the candle sitting between us. Her blonde hair was loose with a slight curl at its tips, her eyes all the more blue for the aqua-coloured dress that hung loose on her curves. I was still as crazy about her as the first time we met a little short of four years ago. She caught me looking and smiled. "What are you thinking?"

"I'm thinking I like it here. This could be a good place for you to paint."

"We'll see."

I reached across and placed my palm on the back of her hand. "You look stunning."

Her smile widened, the way it did whenever I said something nice. Some people can't take a compliment, but that's one thing you couldn't say about Maisie. "You're so sweet."

"I mean it. You're beautiful."

She turned her hand in mine and gripped it. Her eyes became a little watery and I glanced at her neck, her shoulders, her tanned arm stretched across the table where our fingers entwined, and at the bandage, so crisp and white against her wrist.

***

It was Maisie's idea to visit Hydra after we watched a documentary about Leonard Cohen's life on the island during the 'sixties when he spent long days working on poetry under the baking sun and nights getting drunk beneath the Greek moon and putting music to his words for the first time. "Hey, we should go there," she said as the credits rolled.

"Sure." I was up for it; we both love Cohen and the little Greek island looked very cool.

"Can you take another couple of weeks off?"

"Of course," I said, thinking she meant some vague time in the future. "It's the perk of being my own boss." We were at her place, our limbs entwined on the sofa. I'd taken a week off work to be with Maisie after her hospital discharge, and we spent the time watching films and reading. She hadn't been down to her basement studio yet, but her mood had improved and I was hopeful. Although painting could become all-consuming for her, it was also the one thing that kept her from the precipice.

"Great! We'll go next week."

"Uh, okay." I'd begun to learn how it was with Maisie; all or nothing, up or down, now or never. The ups were as dangerous as the downs, and she would sometimes work on a canvas for two days with little food or sleep before collapsing in bed, exhausted. There had been a big exhibition of her work in London and New York at the turn of the year – abstracts inspired by women in history – and it was in the lull after as she struggled to find a new theme that it went downhill this time around. The trip could be good, I thought, for both of us. The thing about loving somebody with a propensity for self-harm is that you become terrified of leaving them alone for a single second. I pulled her close, took in the scent of her hair that I knew I could identify blindfolded in a packed room of women. "I'll sort out the arrangements."

***

"Imagine. Leonard sitting up there on his terrace, notepad on his lap, black sunglasses, a cigarette hanging from his lips."

I followed Maisie's gaze up the white stone walls. "Marianne sunbathing by his side," I said.

"God, she was beautiful. No wonder he wrote such a great song about her."

"Every artist needs a muse."

Maisie smiled at me. "You know that you're mine, don't you?"

"You haven't painted me yet."

"Maybe I never will." She took a sip from her bottle of water. The autumnal heat was good, not too hot to bear. "But it's always your opinion I think of, whenever I'm working on something. Always what you'll think of it, whether you'll like it or not."

"Really?" It was news to me, and I was flattered.

Maisie nodded. "I don't give a shit what the critics say. Not anymore."

"You shouldn't take too much notice of my opinion. I knew nothing of art until I met you."

"But you know what you like. When you really love a painting you say it's great, and when you hate something you say it's nice."

We laughed a little. "Forever the diplomat," I said. We looked at the house a while longer before heading down the narrow lane back to the sea-road.

"So what's your favourite Cohen song, if you had to pick?"

"Famous Blue Raincoat," I said.

"What about Hallelujah?"

I shrugged. "It'll outlive everything else. But I like the intimacy of the other song." I didn't ask Maisie hers, I knew it already. We passed a man with a donkey carrying goods in saddlebags up the hill. He gave it a pat and said something soothing that the beast acknowledged with a flick of its long ears.

"I may do a little sketching later."

"Great."

"I feel inspired. This island is full of good ghosts."

I sensed it too. Something electric, yet soothing, permeating through the atmosphere, spreading good intentions. Maybe it was just the sea and the light, and the pervading quietness. We came to a bluff of grey ragged rock that sloped in layers to waves lapping gently at the island, and rounded it to a cove where we sat on the sea wall, our feet dangling over the clear surface. We could see to the bottom, where shoals of fish glittered among the stones. Further out, the water turned a forever deepening emerald towards the horizon. I put my arm around Maisie's waist.

"How deep is it?" she asked.

"I don't know." I recalled the title of her favourite song. "A thousand kisses, maybe."

"That's deep enough to drown." I felt her shiver, and she leaned into my embrace and kissed the side of my mouth. "I want to make love," she said. "Come on." She took my hand and we strolled under the afternoon sun to the hotel as if we had all the time in the world.

***

We ate in a taverna built into a low cliff that evening, and shared a bottle of wine, though we were already drunk on the afternoon's activities. After an hour or so of rolling over and under and in and out of each other until our bodies were slick with sweat, Maisie had set up her easel in the corner of our room and begun to paint me as I lay naked on the creased sheets, the window slats throwing diagonal lines across my body. I watched her as she worked. Her eyes were alive again, concentrated and wonderful, and by the time we went for dinner she was relaxed, and optimistic for the first time in a while.

"I have some ideas," she said, between bites of calamari.

"For your art?"

"Yes."

"You have a new theme?"

She wrinkled her pretty little nose. "Sort of. It's a bit fuzzy, but I can feel it forming." It was the way Maisie worked. Some artists paint or sculpt as they feel their way from one subject to another but Maisie was definitely of the school that grabbed an idea and saw it through, whether that took months or even years.

"Can you tell me?"

"It's to do with time, and place."

"Interesting."

She gazed out at the night. "When we leave this restaurant, it will still be here. The tables, the chairs, it will all still exist." I didn't interrupt, I could see she was working her way through something, speaking aloud so she could look at the idea and poke it around. "If Einstein is right, and there's no better theory at the moment, space and time are inextricably linked." She sipped her wine and looked at me. "So every event, every moment, still exists somewhere in space-time, even though we've moved away from it."

I was familiar with the theory. "God. Does that mean there is still a me out there somewhere making all my mistakes, or embarrassments, or grieving for my parents?"

"Yes, but there's also a you out there falling in love for the first time, or partying with your friends, or being treated to ice-cream in the park by your mum and dad."

"Maybe that's what ghosts are."

She shrugged. "Maybe."

***

We made love again that night, this time slow, our faces close as we clung to each other in the darkness, the intimacy driving us to a mutual, tender climax. After, laying in the silver moonlight, we whispered and laughed until silence crept into the room, smothering wakefulness with its soft caress. The discussion at dinner influenced my dreams, and I found myself back at infant school, the faces of long-forgotten classmates surrounding me in vivid technicolor, their voices high and excited, and then I was at the zoo with my parents and sister, then at the cinema with my first girlfriend. I woke a little after two, thirsty and hot, and swigged from the bottle by my side. As I turned to settle back down I noticed the opposite side of the bed was empty, and looked at the bathroom which was unlit, then the small balcony. Maisie was gone. I was suddenly awake, my mind racing through possible scenarios for where she could be as I pulled on the clothes I'd left scattered around the room. I remembered her reply when I told her the Aegean Sea was a thousand kisses deep, and rushed from the hotel.

The island was dark with very few windows lit, and as I left the promenade behind for the cove where we'd sat earlier I relied on moonlight to find my way, and minutes later came to the wall. What was I hoping to find? Was I expecting to see Maisie balancing on the edge, coming to her senses when she saw me? She wasn't there, and I peered at the black depths below. My heart was pounding and I tried to think where else she might have gone, but I knew. This was the place. My body began to shake and I hugged myself, my eyes screwed tight, and something rose from my stomach that felt like a scream.

"Jack?"

I spun, peered back along the dirt path, saw a figure emerge from the shadows. "Maisie?"

She rushed to me, held my face in her hands. "What are you doing here?"

"Maisie." I tried to say more but my throat caught.

"Shh." She stroked my hair and kissed me. "It's okay."

"I woke, but you weren't there." My face was wet, my voice trembling. "I thought—"

"I was there all the time. I heard you leave the room and followed you down here. I was calling you, you must have been dreaming, or sleepwalking."

"But . . ." I was going to say I've never been a sleepwalker, but dropped it. Maybe this time I did sleepwalk. Or maybe she was lying and somehow I'd gotten here before her, the island and its good ghosts working in my favour.

"Oh my God, you thought I was going to do something."

I nodded, unable to reply.

"Oh, Jack I'm sorry, I'm so sorry."

I pulled her close, breathed her in, kissed the top of her head. "You have to promise me, Maisie. Please." My voice cracked. "I can't live like this."

She pulled back and looked at me, kissed me, wiped the tears from my cheeks. "I promise I'll try, Jack. I'll try my bloody hardest. I love you."

We stood there clinging to each other, moving through time at the speed of light, making moments. At last, Maisie slipped from my arms. "Let's sit here awhile." We swung our legs over the wall and gazed upon the endless darkness, our bodies cooling now from the gentle breeze wafting off the sea.

The moon was full and fat, and Maisie tipped her face to it. "Greece is a good place to look at the moon, isn't it?" It was a line from Cohen's poem, *Days of Kindness*.

I followed her gaze. "It is," I said, and hoped our days of kindness were still to come.

IT CAME *CLEO FELSTEAD*

Blood mixes with water
As I say goodbye to my daughter
Or son
I'll never know
As your life was too young.

Nature over took
My body
And
Mind was not over matter,
It was a matter of my womb
Reigning over all

I felt like an animal.

Possessed by urges and openings,
And when I was ready to stop
My body continued
Forces straining to keep harmony

Endurance became a pretence
Following to a desperate plea
For it all to stop
Labour usually delivers a baby
Not for me

Just an ending
To the contents
Of my 9 weeks
Of hope.

Covered in my own blood
The life blood
That might have carried you through

I loved you
Small sac and growing
Tissue

I saw you alive
I saw you not
I will hold my own
You will not be forgot

For this motherhood thing
Cannot be separate
From myself

We grow with our blood
Full of passion and life.
I cannot pass you away
And be the same as yesterday

I suspect I am stronger
Bigger somehow
Three miscarriages on
I'm getting used to it now

But this one hurt
Much more than the others
The odds were on our side
To create sisters or brothers
For our beautiful boy
Whom my womb grew perfect.

Yes I know I am blessed
And its nature taking its course
And I'm so lucky

Blah blah blah.

Don't tell me my grief
Or try to order my feelings
I will decide when hope will return
I will decide when that yearning will burn
Out or explode or disappear
It might be a day
It might be a year
This is all mine
And I am already fine.

As nature calms down in my body
And my mind returns to its civilized capability
I know there are forces
Greater than my thinking.
Not a God for me
But I was taken over beyond this strange
Idea of human reality.

Are we sitting idle
In our comfort?
Unaware of the fires that burn
And control?

Oh beautiful thinking
How easy it is to be just with you
When the soil and the blood and the atoms control
Whenever they want to.

MOTHERHOOD WEEK
130 *CLEO FELSTEAD*

We talk! We actually talk to each other.
About wheels mostly
But sometimes about squirrels and trees
We're not quite at the birds and the bees!
Thank God.
Slow down.

Never have I been so in love
And never have I been
So annoyed
So quickly.

You are only two and a half years young
Doing the things that a two and a half'er should:
Like tipping my make up all over the floor (drat)
Or pulling sodden socks off the sodding clothes horse,
Tossing them about with a galloping glee
For all of your entertained toys to see.

And the swiping off tables, ooo that gets me going
Everything in sight:
Bowls of dried up cornflakes
Chess sets piece by piece.
(I try to have places for things, crayons in Roses tins)

You say:
"No Mum, not a place for everything and everything in its place.
I'm two and a half and everything you adore belongs on the floor."

Put on your trousers and let's get going.
"I don't like clothes today Mum,
or going to the park
or staying upstairs
or changing my nappy."
But parenting isn't about making the parents feel happy
'Cause I'm happy in my heart quite simply that you exist.

You aren't tied down by the hands of our measured clocks
You are free and thoroughly led emotionally
I'm sorry that sometimes I'm not stronger for you
That I am a human too
Cross, impatient and wanting to cry.

I've been kicked in the face as I pushed you on the swing
Had metal cars thrown in rage at me,
Skilfully batted off with an empty potty!

No one told me
I needed self-defence classes
Forget NCT
I needed a black belt in Karate!

And then genuine laughter spills out of you.
And you get a joke and all the conflict just passes away in a light breeze.
You are like sunshine warming through my every vein
Energising the source of me.
Right-sizing me into my human shape.
I'm really not that important.

Silent smiles about nothing much.
Just hello you and hello me.
Yes, we exist and isn't that great.
It can all be so simple and yet
Motherhood can feel so incredibly intense

In the smallest of moments.

I'm bossed about
Snotted on (deliberately),
I sometimes get poo on my fingers,
I've been head butted (it really hurt),
Scowled and whined at
We regularly engage in various textile tugs of war.

But also my hair is twirled absentmindedly,
I'm clung to, a human pillow.
Out of the morning dark the gentlest of voices whispers
"Hello Mum"
And it is pure.

You learn to jump and I jump with you.
I do. I love that.

You won't remember the first time you stood on one leg
Or saw a snail poke out its head
We will, Dad and I.
It's magic.

And as music takes hold of your body
And you dance with the freedom of a tribal warrior
I sit still, watching you grow
Banging a drum to the sound of your feet
You becoming the rhythm of my pounding heartbeat.
Motherhood week 130.

MOTHERHOOD WEEK
182 *CLEO FELSTEAD*

Sitting on a bench in the rain
Watching our umbrella fly away
The long summer grass
Shadowed by the looming storm.

Silent smiles
Understanding
No words
My boy

The twinkle in your eye
Gleams like sunlight on
The rippling brook
Where searching hands delve
To find stones to throw

Splashes
Shrieks
Misplaced water
My boy

Sometimes I know which
Animal you will choose next
And I remember that once
You were a part of me

Attached
Extended outwards
To be held and set free
My boy

Rain runs
From the mountain that
First caught it.

I watch you grow
Away from me
Quite rightly so,
And my love won't always be
Allowed to be as close
As it is now

Seeping
Overflowing
Hand received
My boy

Oh, to envelope this time
This magical
Exhausting
Intimate time
And keep it safe
From memory's
Loose grip.

Yoghurt still smears
Across your face
But you can fasten
Your own shoes.
You think answering
Everything with the word
Poo is hilarious.
You are right
My boy.

I am clambered upon
A human climbing frame

Your skins contact feels
Like a homecoming

Pure
Complete
The truth
My boy

To have grown you
And fed you with
My body
Of which you were a part,
A part which I can love
So freely.

But a mother's shining
Cross to bear;

You do not belong to me

You are your own man
To become
And separate we shall be
You should separate from me.
But attached forever
I will be.
My love
My boy.

IN THE SYMPHONY OF LIGHT *IAN D BROWN*

It was the type of night you would rather be inside than out. Darkness was rapidly closing in and the elements were doing their worst.

As the howling wind lashed the rain against the solitary window the last of the four men dragged his chair to the centre of the cold room and sat on it, hands clasped, facing the other three around an old wooden table. The dim lightbulb above was just enough to keep the pitch-black outside. "Well, where do want me to start?"

"The beginning's never a bad place, Frank."

"Hmm the beginning." His voice was deep and dry, gravel pit dry. The type of sound you can only achieve after smoking forty cigarettes a day for most of your life, chasing it down with the strong stuff. He placed an old, battered tobacco tin on the table and carefully lifted the lid before rolling himself another one. "Well, as far back as I remember it's only ever been one way. My parents were Irish Catholics. Not to say I ever had much use for confession, though. I never saw the inside of a church. And didn't much believe in God either. I believed I was the master of my own destiny. My old man, when he was around, was a drunk most of the time. That's if he wasn't banged up or on the run from the old bill. And as for my old lady, she wasn't much better. Well let's just say she wasn't exactly the maternal type. I was fending for myself as early as I could remember. First thing I ever nicked was a rubber at school. I couldn't have been no more than four or five, it was in the shape of a car. I can see it just as plain now as I'm looking at you three. I just wanted it. It was like this feeling just came over me and I had to have it. So I waited until the teacher turned her back to talk to one of the other kids. Then I grabbed it off her desk and put it straight in my pocket. It felt good, really good, like I'd achieved something. And from that moment on I was hooked. It was like that with violence, in a way, after I knocked the local bully into next week. My prize was a half-smoked cigarette from my old man, which made my eyes water more than any punch I took in the fight." They laughed at that, and he took a long drag on his cigarette before blowing smoke towards the ceiling.

"Well, growing up from my background, you didn't have any choice, it was in your blood, it's just the way it was, as if your life was already mapped out. Burglaries, robberies, dodgy deals, violence, nice cars, and fast women. Sometimes it was the other way round, but only sometimes." He smiled and took another drag. "It was all part of the same thing, a means to an end, another fix until the next one, until you hit the jackpot. Then there was prison. Prison was just like a holiday camp. You met up with all your mates and planned your next job. A piece of piss. This was fast life as they called it. And I was in the outside lane. But you know what they say. There's always one last job. That special one. The one with your name on it. The one that sets you up for rest of your life that makes everything worthwhile. And makes all the pain disappear."

TWELVE MONTHS EARLIER

> London Evening Press
> KILLER FREED EARLY
>
> *Convicted double murderer Franklin Gregan is released from prison today after the appeal court found in his favour on a technicality after serving only two years of a life sentence. Gregan, 60, had previously been convicted of the double murder of Lord and Lady Chumley-*

Brown in a botched burglary at their mansion home in the picturesque village of Castle Combe in the Cotswolds. The elderly couple surprised the intruders after coming home early from an evening out...

There must have been about a dozen reporters at the main gate. So, they smuggled me out first thing while it was still dark through the side entrance. I didn't know whether she'd be there or not, but there she was. Just as she said she would be. It was the first time I'd seen her in the flesh. She said she didn't want to visit me inside, but it was definitely her. No mistaking that. I'd gone over the description she sent to me enough times. She was slim. Short cropped blonde hair. Piercing blue eyes behind large round framed glasses. Hands inside of her bright red trench mac. She was like a beacon of light in the dim dawn and looked every bit as good as the fresh smell of freedom.

"I didn't think you'd be here, Lizzie."

"What made you think that? I told you would be," she said. "And I always keep my promises."

It was a year to the day since I received her first letter: the prison was running a pen-pal scheme. The governor thought it would help with our rehabilitation, especially 'lifers' like me. So, I thought what the fuck, in for a penny in for a pound. It'll look good on my record, and a bit of female company. What's not to like? I wasn't sure whether to hug her or kiss her on that first meeting. In the end, it was a bit of a quick, awkward handshake.

"So, where to now?" I asked.

"I booked a car." She gestured further down the road to a parked car with its lights on. Nice ride 'Schumann Chauffeurs'. You see I can't forget a name, I've got a bit of a photographic memory for things like that. Well, in our line of business it pays to recognise names and faces. "We can go to my place," she said. We jumped in the back and off we went. In her letters she said she lived in a bedsit in Bayswater and worked as a cleaner in some posh house in the country. We didn't speak much on the journey, I didn't really know what to say which was a bit unusual for me, I can tell you. I do remember the radio was playing some type of classical music. I remember her asking me once in her letters whether I knew anything about classical music. I said I didn't have a clue. The driver seemed to know his way well, twisting and turning through the dim backstreets. We seemed to get there in no time. The car stopped outside of a three-storey house with black metal railings. Set in a row of some tatty old Edwardian terraces. Mozart Mansions it said on the sign.

She paid the driver, and in we went through the main door past an old balding grey-haired night watchman on reception. He nodded to her but said nothing to me. Three flights of stairs and at the end of a long narrow corridor she pulled keys out at the very last door. "Don't expect anything too fancy," she said. As if I'd been used to anything fancy. The room was small but sparse. Hardly looked as if anyone was living there at all, a single bed, an old wooden chair next to a three-drawer dresser with a load of newspapers on top and a pile of books on the floor. There was a strong smell of perfume I didn't notice it in the car. It must have been all the excitement, but it was strong in the room. I'd smelt it before on the crisp typewritten letters she sent to me. I used to hold them to my nose in bed at night and imagine what she looked like.

"I'll get you some tea, take a seat." She disappeared into a tiny kitchen. The papers on the dresser were all yesterday's. Times. Telegraph. Independent. Daily Express. The books were neatly piled on top of one another. Dracula. Frankenstein. Moby Dick. Dr Jekyll and Mr Hyde. Top of the pile was the Count of Monte Cristo with a bookmark near the end. She came into the room holding two cups. "There you are, white with four sugars. I remembered."

"Can I smoke?"

She pointed to a no smoking sign above my head. "Those things are going to get you into a lot of trouble one day," she said.

That first meeting we must have spent the best part of a couple hours, mostly small talk, but I told her amongst other things it was her letters that I looked forward to. The prison service had sorted me out with some digs across the other side of town. We exchanged details and promised to stay in touch.

Over the next months it was pretty easy going. We spoke on the phone. Met at a local cafe a few times. She was a cool customer alright. And I liked her. Now listen. I've had more than my fair share of women in my time. Good, bad, and somewhere in-between. But I never met one quite like Lizzie before. There was something about her. The packaging looked plain on the outside to the untrained eye. But there was something a little different about her. She had a hidden class. A way about her. The way she walked. The way she talked. The way she sat. Even the way she smelt. I'm not even sure if she even knew it herself. Maybe it was all that time spent working at that big country house with the lady of the manor that had rubbed off on her. But it was definitely there. I could sense it.

Now I don't want you to get the wrong idea. She was young enough to be my daughter. Our relationship was strictly platonic, but slowly I started to get to know her a little better. She was a strange one. A bit of a mystery. An only child, unmarried, lived alone. A bit of a loner. She wasn't much of a talker, either. She had a very slight accent I couldn't quite place. And didn't speak much about her past. She did say her parents had died when she was young and that she was adopted at six. It was difficult to get behind her guard, but I sensed she was hiding something. Some deep pain. I don't think I ever saw her smile. I once asked her why she decided to write to me.

"None of us can escape our destiny," she said.

Well I'd been out a nearly a year and had a few ideas, but I was keeping my head down for the time being. Then, out of the blue, it happened. Lizzie called me up one morning and asked if we could meet at a cafe in the afternoon near where she was living. "Sure," I said. When I got there, she was sitting at her usual table in the corner. We ordered tea, made a little small talk, and that's when she hit me with it. She said she wasn't sure if she should tell me, but she trusted me. I could tell from the look on her face it was something really big. She asked if I'd ever thought about things being different. "Different? What do you mean, different?" I said.

"Different scenery, a different life. Getting away from all of this. Never having to worry about money again." Storybook of my life, I was thinking to myself. "Go on," I said. She started to explain. She said the lady of the house where she worked, the recently widowed Lady Brahms-Dvorak, was very rich, and a couple of weeks ago a man had come to the house for a private meeting with the lady. This man, a Mr Haydn, was a close friend of the lady, and had visited the house on a few occasions before. She said he worked for a firm of auctioneers and had come to take a look at some valuables. Those valuables were jewels. Mr Haydn, she said, was an expert in his field. Lizzie had overheard their conversation through an opened window while picking flowers in the garden that she was preparing for a bouquet. Mr Haydn had valued the jewels at five million pounds. Now, that's when she got my full attention.

Five million pounds.

I asked her if she was sure. "Yes," she said. He had mentioned the figure twice. The lady was planning to auction the jewels and invest the money in a business venture. Lizzie knew where the jewels were kept and had remembered the combination of the safe written on a piece of paper when the lady had it installed a few months before. And was certain the same combination was being used. If I agreed to help this could be the answer to all our problems. She had a plan and if I was interested, we should move quickly, as the jewels would be going to auction next month. As she explained everything, she looked me straight in the eye, and didn't flinch once. She was as cool as cucumber, as if she'd been planning this all her life. We finished our tea and agreed to meet again soon.

For the next few days, I couldn't think of anything else. It just kept going around and around in my head, day and night.

I never expected anything like this. But I always felt there was something she wasn't telling me. Five million pounds worth of jewellery sitting in a country house in a safe with a combination number at my fingertips. All of a sudden that feeling came over me again. You know, the one I had in school as a kid all those years ago. I had to have it. I was in. But what was the plan? How would she get away with it and what part exactly would I play in all of this? The next time we met was at her bedsit one Friday evening. This time there was no sign of the old boy on reception. It felt like we were the only ones in the whole building. Her small room was immaculate as usual, with her favourite classical music playing softly in the background. She put two teas on top of the dresser. "You can smoke if you wish."

"You sure?"

She nodded and sat with her legs crossed on the edge of the bed, in a light blue floral dress looking every bit the English lady. She passed over a small saucer for the ash and explained everything. The lady of the house would be away for few days on business, and she'd been asked to keep house over the weekend. Most of the staff would be on leave so there would only be a skeleton crew. Herself and the elderly gardener, Mr Grieg. Over the next half an hour I sat there captivated as she mapped the whole thing out from start to finish. "Well, what do you think?" she said.

"What do I think? I think, if you pardon my French Lizzie, that it might just fucking work."

The cab journey back to mine went by in the blink of an eye. My head was filled with what I'd just heard. It might just fucking work. But one part of the plan troubled me. Something I had to do, that I'd never done before. But it was essential to make everything look genuine and keep Lizzie away from suspicion. I was struggling with it but it had to be done. In fact, it was absolutely essential.

Everything was agreed. There were no more meetings, and I wouldn't see her again until D-day. The plan was set and I knew exactly what I had to do.

Finally, the day came. I was feeling good, and I set off in the middle of the night. The journey down to the west country seem to fly by. An old acquaintance had set me up with a motor. False plates, nothing too flashy. Nothing that was going to attract attention and get me stopped, but good enough to get me there and back without breaking down.

The directions were spot-on. I turned onto an old slip road and parked in a lay-by at the edge of the woods, shut the engine off and killed the lights. It was pitch black. Three-thirty-five am exactly. About twenty yards ahead was the pathway she told me about. A few minutes later I was on the other side in a clearing at the edge of a large field. Yeah. there was the sign.

PRIVATE PROPERTY. TRESPASSERS WILL BE PROSECUTED!

The grounds of the mansion bordered the fields. In the distance I could just about make out the shape of the mansion. Once on the grounds I crept past an old out-house where old Mr Grieg lives. No worries there, though, he sleeps like a log. Lizzie always made him a night cap before bedtime but tonight there would be a little something extra in his cocoa besides his two sugars. Sweet dreams old boy. The servant's quarters backed onto the mansion and, just as she said it would be, the lower window of the bedroom was left ajar. Although I knew what was coming, I still got that feeling. You know, the feeling we all get just before any job. But this time it was different. Maybe because I knew what I had to do next.

In through the window, and there she was laying there in bed as still as the night, covered in white linen sheets with her back to me. That's when my heart really started to race. I crept up, slowly peered over. The sheets flew back, and she leapt at me screaming, both hands towards my face. Whack! I smacked her with a backhander and put her straight back down. She lay motionless but that was all part of the plan. The part I didn't want to do, the part I'd never done before, but the part I had to do to make it look legit. I hit her hard enough to put her down and probably bruise her but no more. I took a bottle out of my bag and poured a little chloroform on a cloth which I left beside her on the pillow. Her eyes were closed. I fought the urge to speak. We said nothing. It was better that way. I shut the door behind me. Now, the easy part. I'd memorized the layout. A few long corridors led me to a door that opened into the massive reception hallway. The crystal chandelier was the size of my car. Old portrait pictures lined the spiral staircase up to the first-floor bedrooms.

The lady's master bedroom was like something out of Buckingham Palace, but there was no time for sightseeing. Suddenly I got the feeling I was being watched. A huge portrait of some old bloke hung above the fireplace, and the bugger's eyes were fixed right on me. Ludwig Van Beethoven 1770 - 1827. He had a look on his face as if he knew something I didn't. Behind the big portrait is where the safe was located. Now the combination made sense. Seventeen to the left. Seventy to the right. Eighteen to the left. Twenty-seven to the right. BINGO!

Couldn't be easier. Five million pounds worth of jewellery staring me straight in the face. Once they were out, I smashed up the safe a bit, fiddled the lock to make it look right, then trashed a few other rooms on the landing. I waved goodbye to Ludwig on my way out. Couldn't have been any easier. Retraced my steps back to the car.

On the drive back, all I could think about was Lizzie laying there on the bed. Well, that and about five million burning a hole in my bag. I'm sure she was alright. The plan was first thing in the morning she'd make her way down in a sorry state to Mr. Grieg, who'd call the old bill. Lay it on nice and thick. Say she'd been attacked by robbers in the middle of the night. The week before the robbery she had informed the police that she had seen a suspicious man lurking in the fields. The description she gave would lead them on a wild goose chase. Weeks later, once everything had cooled down a bit, she'd inform Lady Brahms-Dvorak that she couldn't cope and that the stress of what she'd been through was too much for her to carry on. We'd meet up.

By which time I'd have sold the jewels and we'd split the money between us. The plan was absolutely perfect. Except for one small detail. It was perfect for her.

***

The three men who were totally transfixed by every word they were hearing flinched backwards, widening their eyes in a mixture of shock and anticipation. They looked at each other, stunned. Frank reached into his top pocket and pulled out a creased page from an old newspaper and unfolded it on the table.

All three leaned closer to the page and peered at it. The youngest of the three rocked back onto his chair, clasping his face. The other two looked at each other, open mouthed.

"Fuck. In. Hell. No fucking way, Frank. No fucking way. Now that's what I call one twisted bitch."

Frank nodded. "Yeah, and I'm the one who tied the first knot. They say revenge is the strongest of all emotions. And she certainly played me hard. Played me hard like a violin in an orchestra."

The men shook their heads in disbelief.

London Evening Press
BEAST RECAGED

Career criminal Franklin Gregan was back behind bars last night.

Gregan, 60, released earlier this year after serving only two years of a life sentence for murder, was sent down at the Old Bailey late last night, convicted of aggravated burglary. Shockingly, the victim, Eliza Chumley-Brown, 27, was the adopted daughter of Lord and Lady Chumley-Brown, for whose murder Gregan had been released early on a technicality. Gregan was tracked down after his DNA was found at the property on a half-smoked cigarette he carelessly discarded. It isn't known whether Ms Chumley-Brown was deliberately targeted by Gregan, or if it was just a cruel twist of fate.

The Belarusian born heiress, a huge classical music fan who inherited her late adopted parents' billion-pound fortune, is the owner of multiple businesses and a huge property empire. When asked how she now felt about Gregan, she answered quietly, "You can't escape your destiny."
Gregan will be detained at Her Majesty's pleasure and may never see the light of day again.

The picture of Eliza in the newspaper showed her with dark hair, brown eyes, and no glasses.

***

"She set whole thing up. The letters. Her story. The plan. The people. The names. The disguise. Everything. She even kept the cigarettes I smoked and planted them at the scene. "Those things are going to get you into a lot of trouble one day," she said. "And you can't escape your destiny."

"She was right." Frank rolled himself another cigarette, and a loud bang on the metal door startled the four men.

"Bedtime ladies," a loud voice bellowed from outside. "Lights out. That's enough for one night. We'll be open again tomorrow, usual hours. It's not as if you've got anything else better to do, is it?"

The warden's laugh echoed in the old Victorian brick hallway outside the cell. He gave the door another bash with his baton and continued on his round.

"Bastards!" shouted the youngest of Frank's cellmates.

The four inmates sat for a moment, before making their way back to their bunk beds as the lights went out.

"Sleep well boys. Same time, same place, tomorrow."

"Yeah, sleep well Frank."

Frank sat on his bunk and took a Bible from under his pillow. He opened it at the bookmark and read the passage quietly to himself.

> *John 1:5*
> *"The light shines in the darkness, and the darkness has not overcome it."*

HUMAN LIMITATION *ANA CASTELLANI*

Self-limiting chaos – the nonsense of our present lifetime
Discussions for the sake of passing time
Pretending to care, faking to understand
The forced allowances that forgive our meaning.
No peace.
No rest.
Just thoughts of a reward we deem to deserve.
Behind a glass of wine, we find our futility
Funny because it's never been lost – just hidden from conscious thought
And there we go again.
We're constantly searching.
All pointless disappointment
There is no purpose
We're all just wasting burrowed time.

A LIFE FOR A LIFE *ROBERT WILLIAMS*

He could see nothing through the windscreen apart from the rain-blurred impressions of red tail lights in the distance. Occasionally some of them would flare as drivers hit their brakes and others darted around like a slow firework display. His eyes were fixated on the view ahead of him and so he was surprised when he looked at his speedometer.

"Forty!" he shouted out loud. He would never get there on time at this rate. "I can't keep you waiting, can I, Francine?"

His foot nudged the accelerator gingerly and his speed slowly increased. Fifty. It wasn't safe, but he felt he could manage it. He didn't want to be late. He would just have to be careful. It was only rain, after all.

Without warning, a yawn erupted from his lips. He looked at the clock. It was after midnight.

"Damn," he said to himself. "No wonder I'm tired."

He could feel the warm fuzzy feeling of impending sleep trying to close his eyes and he shook his head to fend it off, like a dog shaking off water, trying to stay focussed on what he could see of the road ahead. He blinked and then blinked again, slower. Closing his eyes seemed so tempting.

The rasp of his car's tyres hitting the rumble strip woke him and he shook his head again. He hadn't even noticed he was falling asleep.

"Bloody hell," he thought. "That was close. I shouldn't be doing this."

He laughed. Of all the things he had done, driving while dangerously tired was not the worst. It wasn't even close.

Just then a large blue sign loomed up out of the rain. Services 2 miles.

"I'll stop for a coffee. It'll still be open," he said out loud. "Might give the rain a chance to ease off as well."

***

The services were busier than he expected. He'd thought he'd be the only customer but there were a handful of other drivers, mostly truck drivers by the look of them, sheltering from the rain and drinking extra-strong coffee. A group of them sat together, exchanging horror stories about bad drivers. Occasionally they would erupt into loud laughter.

A bored boy in an anonymous coffee shop was serving coffee and pastries and an equally bored older man in an otherwise empty shop was selling sweets and yesterday's newspapers. Adrian bought a paper from him and a triple espresso from the boy.

He sat at a table well away from the group of truckers, but he was not completely alone. Some of the neighbouring tables were occupied by similar single drivers but they were absorbed in books, newspapers, or their phones. He was satisfied he wouldn't be disturbed.

The coffee was too hot to drink but impatience made him try and he burned his tongue. The newspaper's front page was dominated by yet another story about Necro Jack. There had been another murder, it said, bringing the total to twenty-five. No-one was safe. He smiled at that. Typical newspaper sensationalism. Nonetheless, he read the rest of the article, occasionally tutting and blowing on his still too hot coffee.

"Excuse me, mate. Any chance of a lift to Manchester?"

Adrian hadn't heard the man walk up to his table. Nor had he heard him speak to any of the other drivers. His voice was distinctive, rough, like he needed to cough, and Adrian would have noticed if the man had spoken to anyone else first.

He had an accent that Adrian couldn't place. It sounded fake, which made Adrian suspicious. Not that Adrian would give him a lift in any case. He never trusted hitchhikers. And besides, Francine was waiting. He'd wasted enough time already. He could delay no more. He would have to drive faster to make up the time.

"Sorry," he said. "I'm not going that far."

"Then how far are you going?"

"Nowhere you want to go."

"Ah, come on. It's pissing down. I need to get h—"

"Sorry. I just don't pick up hitchhikers."

The man glared at him and walked off, dripping as he went. Adrian shrugged and took a cautious sip of coffee. It had cooled so he took a longer gulp. He looked up again to see if the man had had any luck with any of the other drivers, but he had gone.

"Good job," said a man at the next table. "You can't be too careful these days." He tapped his newspaper. The same Necro Jack headline was on view.

Adrian laughed. "You can't believe all those stories."

"Oh, they're real enough. My brother is a copper. He knows all about it."

"There are really twenty-five victims? Sounds too many to me."

The trucker shrugged. "They're not sure. Could be more."

"Your brother's pulling your leg. They've got that many bodies?"

"You've got me there. I don't know."

"Then they're just missing persons."

"What gets me is that he is so random," said the other driver, obviously not wanting to let a good story drop. "Takes pretty girls and great big blokes as well."

"Really?"

"It was on the news. Big strapping lads they were. Killed and then raped just like all the others."

"Raped?"

"You know what I mean. He shags the bodies afterwards."

"I'll try to be careful. He won't catch me."

"I make sure I lock my cab properly at night."

Adrian took a long look at him before replying. The man was sporting one of the last combovers in Britain and it was in desperate need of a wash. So was his t-shirt which was stretched to bursting point by his stomach and was decorated by numerous food stains.

"I think you'll be ok," he said, with a laugh in his voice.

The man smiled thinly, and Adrian wondered if the insult had even registered. He shrugged, not caring, and stood up. The coffee and the brief rest had done the trick. He needed to go. Francine was waiting.

***

The rain was still pouring heavily as Adrian reached the exit. He pulled his collar up and steeled himself for the run to the car. It was parked close to the building, but he knew he would be soaked all the same.

"Don't move." He heard the voice at the same time as he felt something poking him in the back. "I've got a knife."

Adrian recognised the voice. The phoney accent was unmistakable. It was the man who had wanted a lift.

"I don't have any money," he said.

"I don't want money. I just need transport."

Panic suddenly washed over Adrian. His car! The man wanted his car! He couldn't let him have it. Francine!

"Don't take my car. Please mate. Don't take it."

The voice behind him laughed. "I don't want your car. I just want it to take me somewhere."

Whatever was pointing at his back dug in a bit harder, forcing him to move out into the rain and walk to his car. Adrian didn't want to risk running. The upturned collar made no difference. Water streamed down the back of his neck and his clothes clung to him like a cold second skin.

"You really want to go to Manchester?"

"You'll find out."

Adrian unlocked the car and reached out to open the

driver's door.

"No. Give me the keys. I'll drive."

"What?"

"I'll drive. Get in the passenger side."

Adrian turned to face him, determined to stop him driving off in his car. He couldn't allow that to happen. He'd never get to see Francine again.

As he did so, the man slapped him in the chest. When he took his hand away, something round, sleek, and black was left behind. It looked, and felt, like a black glass paperweight with lights twinkling deep within it.

"Is that a bomb?"

"No."

"It looks like a bomb."

"Get in the passenger seat."

Adrian backed slowly away and made his way to the other side of the car. He didn't take his eyes off the device, convinced it would explode if he made a sudden movement or touched it. Only when he reached the passenger door did he look up to see the man watching him. He was laughing at him.

"It really isn't a bomb, you know," he said. "Get in."

Both men opened their doors and got in the car. Adrian sat down with exaggerated care, not believing the other man's word.

"It's not a bomb."

"I don't believe you."

The other man shrugged as he turned the ignition key. The radio started up and the man nodded approval at the tune as if he'd recognised an old favourite. Adrian didn't know it. It sounded modern. The man reached up to put on his seat belt and Adrian, out of habit, went to copy him.

"No. Leave it off."

"What?"

"No belt."

"Why? Will it interfere with the bomb?"

"No, but no belt. And, for the love of God, it really isn't a bomb, Adrian."

Rubbish, Adrian thought. It had to be a bomb. He was trapped in a car with a madman who had stuck a hi-tech bomb on him, but he wore a seatbelt himself. What did that mean?

Then he realised something.

"You know my name," he said. "You called me Adrian. How did you know my name?"

"I know a lot about you, Adrian. Don't worry about it."

The man started driving and they re-joined the motorway, Adrian's questions ignored. The radio switched to the news. Another story about Necro Jack. The car picked up speed. Thirty, forty, fifty, sixty. Lights flashed past too quickly and Adrian forgot about the bomb.

"That's too fast. You'll kill us."

"I won't."

Adrian frowned, unsure what to say. The man was clearly insane. The speedo reached somewhere between sixty and seventy miles per hour and stopped.

"Sixty-seven point three, in case you're wondering."

"What?"

"Our speed. Sixty-seven point three miles per hour."

"That's very precise," he said in a voice that was calmer than he felt. He really wanted to scream at the man to slow down.

"We need to make up some time."

Time? Did he know about Adrian's date with Francine? How? Why would he be helping him?

"Where are you taking me?" he asked. The other man laughed but didn't answer.

Adrian was aware that they moved to avoid other cars but, at this speed, he wouldn't have even seen them in time.

"Who are you?" he asked. It was an irrelevant question but of the hundreds that were bubbling around his head, it was the easiest to articulate.

"Call me Lewis," the other man answered and turned to shake Adrian's hand. "Pleased to meet you."

Professional habit made Adrian grasp the proffered hand and shake it for a second before the rest of his brain took in the situation. Lewis was not looking at the road! He was driving at seventy in the dark in the rain and was not looking at the road.

"Don't look at me, you idiot! Watch where you're going. You'll get us killed."

In answer, Lewis laughed and closed his eyes, causing Adrian to panic all the more.

"What the fuck are you doing? Open your eyes."

"Ahead of us there is a lorry that is going slower than we are. I will overtake."

Lewis kept his eyes closed while he spoke, but Adrian looked ahead to see a truck's rear lights loom out of the rain just as they swerved to avoid it.

"We will shortly pass a car," Lewis continued, eyes still closed. "It is in the outside lane so I will have to pass on the inside."

Once more, the statement proved to be correct.

"How are you doing this? Are you some sort of psychic?"

Lewis laughed and opened his eyes.

"Good grief, no! There's no such thing."

None of this was making sense and Adrian felt like an actor in a play where he'd been handed the wrong script. He'd been given *Macbeth* while the rest of the world was doing *Carry on Camping*.

"Please let me go. I need to see Francine."

"You'll see her soon enough. Just think of this as a bit of fun."

"Fun? How the fuck can this be called fun?"

"I'm enjoying it."

"When we stop, are you going to let me go?"

"I know you think you will die in this car, but you won't. Trust me."

"Trust you?" Adrian laughed despite his fear. "You've put a bomb on me and—"

Lewis sighed.

"And you're driving like a maniac—"

"Have I hit anything?"

"No. Not yet."

"I won't hit anything unless I plan to. You can trust me."

They drove in silence for a few minutes with Adrian tensing whenever he could see another car ahead of them. His foot automatically stepped on an imaginary brake pedal as they drew closer. It would have been too late had he really been in control of the car but then he would have been driving slower. Probably not much slower, he had to admit, but not at this dangerous pace. And he would have been in control.

"I have implants," Lewis said, ending a few minutes of silence.

"Implants? What?"

"You asked me how I could sense the traffic."

Adrian hadn't used the word 'sense'. He rarely did. The word had all sorts of weird connotations in his mind. Francine wouldn't use a word like 'sense'. She was a librarian. They were too level-headed to use a word like that.

"What sort of implants?"

"Oh, you know, just stuff. Like what you have on your phone but inside my body. A sort of radar, for one thing, knowledge, all sorts."

"This is all rubbish."

Adrian's phone suddenly buzzed in his pocket. He froze. He knew no-one who would call him at this time of the night but whoever it was, he might be able to ask for help.

"Answer it," Lewis said, with a smile on his lips.

Adrian took the phone out of his pocket and looked at it.

"It says it's you."

"Yes."

"But you're not in my address list. How does it know who you are?"

Lewis tapped his nose and winked. Adrian answered the call and Lewis smiled at him from the screen. It was a video call.

"Hello Adrian," Lewis-on-the-phone said. "It really is me."

"How can you do this?" he said to the man in the driving seat.

"Adrian? That's rude. I'm here," said the man in the phone.

"I'm here as well," said Lewis, "but talk to me on the phone for a few minutes."

"This is a recording. Has to be."

"Then how could I know you would look at me? Or, for that matter, how did I know when to call? Or even how I know your name?"

He had no answer for that.

"Speak to me, Adrian."

"This can't be real."

"Oh, it's real. You want me to do something else?"

"Such as?"

"Look outside," Lewis said, and the call ended.

They began passing some electronic road signs that informed them that a lane was closed and that they needed to reduce speed. As he was looking at the signs, they changed.

Hello Adrian, one said.

Do you believe me now, Adrian? read another message spread over four consecutive signs.

He turned to Lewis who tapped himself on the head.

"Implants. Got it now?"

"This is some clever trick."

"Oh, I assure you. It is no trick. The implants are there. We all have them where I come from."

"And where's that?"

"Nonaginta."

"Never heard of it."

"It's a planet."

"Are you off your head? Implants! Another planet! You're insane. Stop the car right now. Let me out."

"No, I can't do that, Adrian. I have something I have to do, and I need you here."

"Why? What have you got planned for me?"

"I can't tell you for the moment."

Adrian tried to open the door, but it was locked.

"Don't be silly, Adrian. Jumping out of a car at this speed would kill you."

Adrian glanced at the speedo. The needle was still hovering steadily on a point somewhere between sixty and seventy miles an hour. It could easily be 67.3.

"Why are you doing this?"

"I've been sent here. I have a mission."

"Your planet is invading us, I take it."

Lewis laughed.

"Nonaginta is a human colony. I'm from the future. 2381."

"Oh no, this is getting worse. Now I know you're mad. How can you be from the future?"

"Stay calm, Adrian. I'm not mad. In fact, that's why I'm here. If I were mad, they'd have fed me a few pills and sent me on my way. No, I'm completely stone-cold sane."

It sounds it, thought Adrian.

"I killed some people."

"What?"

"I was a serial killer."

A chill ran down Adrian's spine. "A killer?"

"You are in no danger from me, Adrian, just listen. It's important."

Adrian ignored him and stared ahead, taking refuge in watching out for the other cars. They dodged another. He was surprised he didn't flinch. Was he believing this insanity?

"When they caught me, I expected to be killed but, instead, I was tried and sent back here."

"You're supposed to kill me as well?"

Lewis laughed.

"No. You will live. Don't doubt it. You'll see."

Adrian continued to stare ahead. If only he'd gone to Francine earlier. It hadn't been possible, of course.

"A life for a life, they call it. I took six lives, so I've been sent back to save yours."

He turned to face Adrian. Despite his new confidence,

Adrian was alarmed.

"You were meant to die in this car today, Adrian."

The comment startled him. Despite all the odd things that Lewis had said, that statement had the most impact.

"I thought you weren't going to kill me."

"I'm not. I said you were *meant* to die. History says you drove too fast in the rain, hit a crashed petrol tanker, and died. But history is wrong."

"Wrong?" How can it be wrong?"

"History says that a man died in your car. It says that your car hit the tanker and burst into flames. The man in the car was only identified as you from his dental records. All of that will still be correct but that man won't be you. It'll be me."

"Why?"

"My sentence. A life for a life. It will happen in a few minutes."

"They'll know you're not me in the wreckage."

Lewis grinned and tapped his teeth with a finger.

"I am your dental double, Adrian."

"What about my DNA?"

"If anything of me survives the fire, it will look like you."

"But you don't look anything like me."

"At the DNA level, I do. Not good enough to clone you but it will fool bog-standard sequencing. They can mess around with your DNA quite a bit in the future. Really fucks you up as well. If I don't die in the crash, then I wouldn't last more than a couple of hours. I already have trouble breathing."

"But what happens to me?"

"You will survive the accident."

"How?"

"I'll send you to the future."

"Again, how?"

Lewis reached across to Adrian and tapped the device on his chest. Adrian had forgotten about it until now.

"Oh. I see. Definitely not a bomb."

"No."

"Then what is it?"

"A time machine of some sort."

"How does it work?"

"No idea. I'm just the delivery guy," Lewis said with a laugh in his voice. The laugh ended in a cough.

"But why did you agree to this? You are killing yourself. Couldn't you have run away when you got here?"

"My implants won't let me do that. I can't deviate from history. And besides, they doctored my DNA, remember. I'm dying."

"You seem very calm about it."

Lewis shrugged.

"Without the implants, I'd be bricking it. Isn't that what you say here? Bricking it?"

"Uh, yeah."

"I chose to kill those people. I have to live with the consequences. We're coming up on the tanker. I need to slow down. You hit it at forty-four point two miles per hour, braking hard but too late."

The rain had cleared just enough for Adrian could see the tanker in the distance. It had overturned and was blocking all three lanes of the motorway. Cars were parked haphazardly in front of it although there was a clear route for his car to get to the tanker.

"Get ready."

"Ready for what?"

The tanker loomed larger in front of them. A man in a high-vis vest – the driver, Adrian guessed – was waving his arms to try to get them to stop. Adrian could feel the brakes coming on hard and heard the squeal of tyres on wet tarmac.

"This."

Lewis slapped the device on Adrian's chest and, just as the car was about to hit the tanker, Adrian's world disappeared.

***

She was dressed in a strange uniform, but it was obvious to

Adrian that she was a nurse.

"Hello Adrian," she said, smiling. "Welcome to 2381. How do you feel?"

The tanker, the car, Lewis had all gone. He was safe. Lewis had been telling the truth. He looked himself over. His clothes were still damp from the soaking in the rain, but he felt fine.

"I'm okay," he said. "At least I think so. This is all a little confusing."

"It will be," she said, smiling. "Time travel can scramble a few neurons."

"Lewis is dead?"

She nodded. "Yes. After he left you at the services—"

"What? He drove me halfway up the motorway. We nearly hit a tanker."

She poked at a small device in her hand and frowned. "He wasn't supposed to do that. I guess we hadn't covered everything in his implants. He still had enough leeway to be a bastard. Our apologies for that."

"That's ok. I survived, after all. I can't complain."

"Good. Now, any headache?"

"No."

"Dizziness?"

"No."

"You hear me ok?"

"Yes, fine."

She smiled and looked at the device again.

"Well, that certainly checks out with what we're seeing. You made the jump intact."

He grinned in relief. "Thank you. Thank you v—"

Her smile faded.

"Magistrate, he's all yours now," she said, and walked away. Adrian seemed to be in an infinitely large dark room. Once the nurse had taken a few steps away from him she was lost in the darkness.

"Magistrate?" he asked, confused.

"Adrian Paul Sampson," said a disembodied voice. "Please

confirm your name for the court."

"Court? I don't und—"

"There needs to be no doubt of your identity. You are Adrian Paul Sampson?"

"Yes, that's me. What's going—"

"Your parents were Derek Michael Sampson and Olivia Jane Hargreaves?"

"Yes."

"Your date of birth was April 19th 1978?"

"Yes. You've got the right man. Now, what's this ab—"

"Adrian Sampson, you are charged here, today, with murder. First witness."

"What? I don't understand."

Adrian heard footsteps behind him, and he turned to face them. A woman stepped into the light and looked him in the eye.

"Francine?" he said, recognising her.

"State your name for the record," the disembodied voice said.

"Francine Jones," she said. Adrian was in shock. Francine was as gorgeous as ever, but it couldn't be her. It just couldn't. He'd left her behind when he'd been pulled into the future. They were to have made love in the Lake District at dawn. Such a romantic setting. It would have been so beautiful.

"What is your relation to the accused?"

"I don't really know him."

"But—" Adrian tried to interrupt. *How could she say that? He loved her.*

"Do you recognise him?"

"He used to come to the library where I worked."

"You didn't speak to him?"

"Just chit-chat."

It was more than that. The words may have meant nothing, but the emotions were there. Francine loved him and he loved her. She knew. That's why he'd kept going back to see her.

"Do you know why you are here?"

"Yes, but I have trouble believing it."

He'd waited until the library had closed.

"Please tell the court what happened from your point of view."

"A woman came into the library just as we were closing. She ... she looked exactly like me. She put some device on my chest. I thought it was a bomb even though she said it wasn't."

He'd hidden himself.

"She took me to the kitchen and put me in a cupboard tied up, but I could still see into the cloakroom. She'd left the doors open just enough."

He'd known her habits and knew she'd go to get her coat.

"At first I was terrified by the bomb. It was counting down. Only a couple of minutes left. Then I saw him. I was going to call to him to help. I ..."

"Please take your time."

"I'm okay, thank you. I'm calm. The pills are working. Anyway, I heard him call out to her. He thought she was me. Of course, he would, she looked exactly like me, after all." She paused to take a breath. "That's when I saw the knife. He stabbed her. Just the once but there was so much blood. I could have stopped him, but I was scared. Of her, the woman who looked like me. Of him, the man who'd stabbed her thinking she was me. Of the bomb stuck to my jumper. But ... but ..."

"Do you need assistance? More medication?"

"No, I'm fine. I need to get all this out or I will never be able to tell you."

The blood had been so red. It matched her hair. She'd looked so beautiful with it framing her body on the floor, like a halo. He'd nearly lost control then but forced himself to keep to the plan. He'd promised her the Lake District.

"As she was dying on the floor, she looked right at me and smiled. Honestly, she smiled and winked. Then the device on my chest started buzzing and I was here."

"You understand what happened now?"

"Yes. I'm on another world in the future. Unbelievable."

"And you know why?"

"Apparently, the woman was a convict. You sent her back to take my place. He," she said, nodding at Adrian, "killed her and put her body in the boot of his car. It would have been me if she hadn't taken my place. He was planning to have sex with my corpse."

She paused and looked Adrian in the eyes before speaking.

"He is Necro Jack."

It had been her. He knew it. She hadn't been a replacement. *This* was the replacement. His Francine was forever changeless. Forever young. Forever beautiful. He'd kissed her as he laid her body in the boot of his car. He knew that had been her. This woman was an imposter. This woman would grow old and ugly.

"Does the accused want to ask questions?" the voice asked Adrian.

He shook his head. What was the point? This woman wasn't Francine, the woman he'd loved and planned to make love to as the sun rose over the mountains.

"Can I ask a question?" Francine asked, suddenly.

"It is unusual. You are a witness and—"

"What will become of me? Can I go home now?"

There was a pause as if the magistrate was thinking how to best answer her.

"I'm sorry but that won't be possible. If we sent you home alive then the past will be changed, and history will be altered. We cannot allow that to happen."

Adrian could see tears in the pretend-Francine's eyes.

"I should be more upset by this," she said, looking at him again. "I should scream and shout and try to claw your eyes out, but they've got me drugged up to the eyeballs to keep me calm. What about my daughter? What about my husband? I've had to leave them behind just because you couldn't keep your dick under control."

"The witness is reminded to keep order in the court."

"What will happen to me?" she asked the voice but there

was no answer. The pretend-Francine stepped back into the blackness, sobbing, and a man stepped forward. Adrian recognised Simon, although it couldn't be his Simon. His Simon was like a god. So handsome. Just like Francine, his Simon would never grow old. He would be beautiful forever.

After Simon, there was Jenny and then Mark and Janice and a dozen others. All fakes taking the places of the beautiful people that he had left behind. They said he'd killed them. Didn't they understand? He'd *saved* them.

Eventually, the collection of 'victims' stopped and there was nothing around him but darkness.

"Adrian Sampson. Do you have anything to say for yourself?"

What could he say? They were wrong? They had all misunderstood. The people who'd spoken were the replacements. His real friends would never have said those things. They'd been so nice to him. So helpful. They had loved him, and he had rewarded them. And there were only seventeen of them. He smiled at the long-forgotten newspaper article in the service station. Twenty-five indeed!

He knew that fighting would make no difference. He knew he was right. He was content to die knowing that.

"No. I have nothing to say."

"Very well. You are hereby judged. Adrian Paul Sampson, you will be taken from this place and prepared for time travel."

There was the unmistakable sound of a gavel hitting a block.

"The sentence is life. A life for a life. Take him away."

WALKING THE BOUNDARY
ALISON BENNETT

In the liminal time I feel the earth breathe,
air damp with growth, wild mangoes and cypress,
the stirrings of creatures, survivors of night.

This is my father's land.

Wild beyond the small patch of grass
to the edge of the boundary pathway,
cut back for his daughter to walk, returning
to the home they've made, so far from the England
of greyness and cold and not-quite belonging
from years of travel.

Each visit I wait for the sunrise
to walk with care through coral and roots,
wait for the shriek of the grackle at first light.
It is our ritual, renewal, a bonding.

My father is gone; my mother is too.
The land is sold.
Now I walk the lost boundary
before waking.

HOW SIGNIFICANT JOURNEYS HAVE IMPACTED MY LIFE *FAY BROWN*

The English dictionary defines Journey as:

i) Travelling from one place to another.
ii) A distance or course travelled.
iii) A period of travel.
iv) Passage or progress from one stage to another.

So, what does this mean? A journey for many people indicates some kind of physical movement from one geographical area to another. Some people like myself enjoy physical travel to different countries in the world where they can experience different cultures, cuisines and environments. I like to travel at least twice a year, visit nice spa centres, and go out for nice meals, I have always gone on exciting holidays abroad to soak up the sun, meet new people, and capture memories from different journeys, such as interesting buildings, cobbled streets, local people making a living and enjoying life. I recognise though, that not all journeys are enjoyable and some can be challenging.

Some physical journeys can be unplanned or unpleasant. For example, walking in bad weather without an umbrella where you end up getting soaked; a long car journey on a motorway which is really congested and slow moving due to a car accident; or travelling on an underground train packed to the brim with passengers, which has to stop in a tunnel without warning for an unknown amount of time.

Not all journeys are physical. We all go through psychological and emotional journeys which can affect our mental well-being and can result in depression, anxiety or suicidal thoughts. Indeed, during this challenging Covid-19 lock-down period there have been many examples of people experiencing depression, isolation, lack of contact with family and friends, loss of jobs, income and businesses. Some minds have been "drenched" with worry and affected by unplanned events which have stopped what were normal routines and daily journeys, physically and mentally. For many people, the train has stopped unexpectedly. Journeys can take different routes and ultimately lead to different places and experiences. I'd like to share three significant journeys I've been on during the last twenty months.

NEAR-DEATH JOURNEY
From November 2018 - present I have experienced a difficult journey and near-death experience. I was diagnosed with pancreatic cancer in December 2018, which I have found is one of the most aggressive cancers. This has become one of the most notable journeys of my life in that it affected my mental and physical well-being. At the onset of being diagnosed I programmed my mind to be mentally and spiritually aware that I was going to overcome the illness and not die, and I would do whatever was required to survive. Some key aspects of this journey included having a very complicated Whipple's operation which removed a part of my pancreas, stomach, gallbladder and a tumour which was resting against a major artery. The operation lasted for over six hours. The key impact of this journey included going through tough chemotherapy sessions, recuperating during 2019, loss of weight, energy and strength, ongoing diarrhoea and stomach aches, reduced mobility, inability to do the things which kept me active such as going to work, the gym, swimming and meeting up with friends.

Despite these difficulties this journey reminded me about

the love of God and the need to stand on faith, and the importance of close family, friends and work colleagues. I re-organised my well-being in terms of eating nutritious foods, nutrients and antioxidants. I had a passion for utilising the services offered at the Guys Cancer Care Centre every time I attended as a patient, and to help other people on my visits. For example, one day while I was having chemotherapy there was a lady in the same unit having treatment, accompanied by her husband. She was upset and agitated. I got talking to them and it turned out they had a very unpleasant journey on public transport getting to the hospital, so by the time they arrived the lady was exhausted before she started her treatment. I asked them why they hadn't used the free hospital transport system. It turned out they didn't know there was such a system they could use, so I gave them the telephone number of the hospital transport department. Two weeks later I met them again at the hospital and they were so happy as they had travelled to the hospital by using the free hospital transport system. They were so grateful to me for giving them the information.

As a result of being a cancer patient at the Cancer Care Centre I was privileged to access services such as free massage sessions which helped my body overcome some of the painful reactions to chemotherapy and my major operation. I also got allocated my own physiotherapist who played a major role in teaching and helping me to recuperate, by tailored exercise routines. The Dimbleby Centre at the hospital connected me to a charity supporting people and their families who are experiencing cancer. The fantastic staff at the Macmillan charity assisted me to get useful advice and help. This near-death journey has made me value life in a completely different way. For example, now simple things matter such as waking up every day with life in my body, having complete faith in the Almighty Lord Jesus Christ, valuing and spending as much time as possible with my kind and loving daughter who took a year out from her busy job as a GP Trainee to support me, not putting off what you want to say or do, not burning my body out at work and valuing my brothers and sisters and friends from church.

COVID-19 LOCKDOWN JOURNEY

The coronavirus pandemic has been a unique journey no one will ever forget. As someone who's been self-isolating following guidance from the NHS, it has been a challenge having to stay indoors. I am someone who traditionally is used to being physically active, driving, going for walks, engaging in social activities and meeting up with family and friends. Covid-19 turned all that around and made me a kind of home prisoner. I also temporarily moved out of my house so I could effectively self-isolate away from my daughter, a medical doctor who on a daily basis has been looking after Covid-19 patients in hospital. However, being the person I am, I was determined at the onset that I would keep myself occupied at home by reading, working from home for two days a week, doing daily exercises, finding a weekly online yoga class, joining in with various zoom meetings and organising family and friends online catch-ups. I even organised a zoom family "drink and dance party" as it was my sister's birthday. I liaised with her on what kind of party she wanted, chose and allocated two DJ's (my brother and nephew), sent virtual invites to key family members reminding them to have their drinks and dancing shoes ready.

One relative attended the party all the way from her sitting room in Florida . . . what a party it turned out to be. Our family literally danced the night away for at least three hours. Nobody wanted to go home. We ended the reggae, soul and blues jamboree with Vera Lynn's famous Song, *"We'll meet again, don't know where don't know when, but I know we'll meet again some sunny day."*

Needless to say, I woke up with a hangover the next day and felt as if I'd run several miles as my body was shattered. What a journey that was. The important thing is that I felt totally energised and closer to my family. Covid-19 lockdown has also led to a resurgence of my skills such as baking cakes, cooking fresh nutritious meals and not being dependent on processed food. I've also learned new ways of communication via online meetings and realised life will not go back to exactly to how it was before Covid-19. This journey has meant that after shielding at home, things will not go back to normal, whatever that means.

A JOURNEY TO THE PARK
Being in lockdown has meant I have stayed indoors for most of the time, apart from sitting outside in our lovely back garden or going for a walk to the local park with my brother. Today I went out for a stroll on my own which has been very rare. Even before I left the house, I was pondering to myself. Should I put my face mask on, or will I look silly as hardly no one now is wearing a mask on the road? But, I thought, I don't care how I look. I'm wearing my mask as I need to protect myself.

In recent weeks the lockdown has been reduced by the government including the reduction of social distancing in public areas, meaning individuals can be nearer to each other. Despite these measures I really don't agree with the corporate message that things are now safer, even though published data indicates a decrease in deaths from the virus. Other measures have included July 4th 2020 "Independence Day" which meant that a variety of different retail units could reopen after several months of closure, such as pubs, hairdressers, barbers, retail shops and restaurants.

As I stepped out of the house a few neighbours at the top of the road waved to me and shouted, *"how are you doing?"* I waved back. I noticed they were having a good chat standing very close to each other with no social distancing. As I walked around the corner, I admired the array of front gardens displaying lovely colourful flowers. I approached the main road and it all seemed normal as if there had been no virus pandemic in recent months. Most pedestrians and drivers had no masks on, including groups of people walking happily together on relatively busy roads. I crossed over and headed for my local park. A single-deck bus drove past me and I noticed everyone I could see on the bus did have a mask on, yet most of the pedestrians who I walked past didn't. There are still dangers in congested spaces such as public transport, and Transport for London has said *everyone travelling on buses and trains should wear face masks*.

The local park is only a five-minute walk from my house. When I entered the park gates I had such a great feeling of liberation, seeing people of all ages jogging, families sitting on the grass having "chill out time", people walking their dogs who themselves looked happy. Mothers pushing their babies in prams. I sat on a bench in what is known as *The Big Field* for a while, and just observed the natural scenery; trees, green grass, and flowers at the front of the houses overlooking the park.

I noticed at one end of the Big Field some children were playing football. Again, most people didn't have masks on, and as I walked past them, I wondered if they thought I was mad for still wearing one. But who cares what they think? You're protecting your life, that's all that matters.

After being in the park for an hour I made my way back home. On the way I walked past someone doing some gardening and weeding at the front of their house as another person arrived home in their car with shopping bags. A tradesman was putting tools in his van after working on the building of my neighbour's new loft extension. I arrived back at my front door and felt a real sense of accomplishment. Once inside I felt like I had knocked down some of the bricks based on my feeling of being a home prisoner, and had overcome some of my fears and achieved something positive just by going for a walk to the local park.

WHAT HAVE I GAINED FROM THESE JOURNEYS?
I'm glad these journeys happened as I wouldn't be the person I am today. First and foremost, I am alive, and I have a different perspective on life and don't take my body for granted and work it to the bone like I used to.

I really value my life and the opportunities to do things I may not have done previously. I really appreciate having "still" time, which enables me to really exercise my mind and spiritual well-being.

I value the natural environment even more so, and the need to step up my game to protect the environment through enhanced recycling and by eating organic vegetables and fruit, as they are healthier for my body, taste nicer, and are not damaging the environment.

I value my daily body exercises which have helped me to regain some of the weight I lost and are building up muscle to my legs and arms. I now cook more healthier nutritionally-based meals and depend less on processed foods.

I've learned new technological online skills such as hosting Zoom meetings. Fundamentally, I am grateful that God has been with me on all these journeys, and has allowed me to share with and give confidence to others, and take away useful experiences I can build on.

DIAMOND SHOWERS *RE CHARLES*

The mirror-ball is a nice touch
To make the boys feel at home
On Saturday nights in the Black Hole Bar
Getting high on synthetic wine and talking about the good old days
Before the cloud rose from Earth
Like a blooming rose

So we laugh and we drink in our orbit-booth
Watching diamond showers over Jupiter's moon
In awe of the beauty that would cut right through
If you got in the way
Which reminds me of a woman I knew
And what I wouldn't give to stroll in the rain with her
One more time

MOVING ON *ALISON BENNETT*

Something was different. The thought was waiting for her as she surfaced. She stretched out her hand and encountered the hard curve of a pelvis, firm belly.

"You're real."

"Of course I'm real."

Ellie didn't need to see Lee to picture his look of amused tolerance. She kept her eyes closed.

"And I'm going to have to get ready for work."

Ellie felt the mattress rise as he got up. "There's clean towels in the cupboard. Help yourself to anything you need."

Ellie sat up when she heard the shower. What should she do? She smiled at that. A fair way through the evening Lee had said, "*Should* is a dirty word."

"And not in a good way." They'd both said it together, their laughter proportional to the alcohol they'd consumed. Oh God. What had she done?

She had to get her act together – he wouldn't be long. Her dressing gown was too ratty for company. She grabbed fresh clothing, hurriedly put it on, not wanting to be caught with one leg in her jeans. Clean clothes, unwashed body. Yuk. But some part of her wanted to keep the trace of him on her skin for just a little bit longer. Teenage thinking, but so what?

***

She managed a (hopefully) confident smile as Lee looked into the kitchen. "Coffee?"

He glanced at his phone. "It'll have to be quick."

They stood, leaning against the counter, close but not very. Ellie tried not to analyse every nuance, to look relaxed.

"You've got some good stuff, smells great." He ran a hand through his close-cropped hair. "Better than my usual."

"Glad you liked it." God, that was inane. And her shampoo was 'colour confidence' so he'd know her hair was dyed. She did a quick mental inventory of her bathroom – always clean so no problem there. But her skincare was on the counter, including the anti-aging moisturiser. In the morning light, she realised that she had five years on him. Maybe ten. And he would realise it too.

Lee finished his coffee, rinsed his mug. "Right, I'm off." He winked as he went out.

Ellie heard the door close and sat heavily on a kitchen chair. Well, what had she expected? Just because they'd got on so well last night, talking for hours before— She gulped the remains of her coffee and stood abruptly. Her friends had egged her on to get back out there, move on. Well, she'd certainly done that. Time to be a grown-up. Shower, laundry, go for a run to lose half a stone a day too late. Maybe clean out the garage. Wash the car. Keep. Busy. She lost track of how long she stood there, clutching her empty mug.

She felt better after a shower. Hadn't thought about Lee in the shower before her. Well, not much.

It was only after the laundry, cleaning the kitchen and another couple of mugs of coffee that she let herself look at her phone. She wasn't expecting a text. Hoping. But not expecting. She couldn't put it off any longer.

Messages from Sarah, John and Helen. And Lee.

Great night. You've got my number now. It's up to you. Lee

Once she'd finished her Snoopy dance, she checked when the message was sent. Ten minutes after he left. Yes! To hell with doing the sensible thing, for once she was going to take a chance. She felt a spike of fear. What *was* she doing? Starting to live again that's what. No promises. No guarantees. She laughed and started to text back.

JOURNEYS HAIKU *HC JOHNSTON*

No-one can step twice
Ever in the same river.
Bright, chill, pure blessing.

Journey's end is clear
In our mind's eye, completion.
But not the answer.

Journeys are what may
Have happened, once, to others.
We are more complex.

ARRIVEDERCI PADRE *LORAINE SAACKS*

"If you want me to pay, you're going to have to go the way I tell you." Sandra hated giving ultimatums but this was more of a cri de coeur.

She pointed to the tabloid open on the kitchen table, "Look at this," she commanded. "Just look … Rome Airport. They put their luggage down for two minutes to buy a cappuccino and when they looked round, zilch, disappeared. And it's endemic they say."

"It's sensationalizing. It happens everywhere. It won't happen to me though. I'm careful," Joel, sixteen. Trying to convince.

1980, and Lucia, a bygone au pair of a close family friend, had offered him accommodation at the family hotel she and her husband now owned. Here, at somewhere on the long, somewhat septic, toe of Italy, Mediterranean side, Joel would be able to perfect his Italian for his 'A' levels. He'd last seen Lucia when he was five, and she was eighteen, but he was certainly game and couldn't wait for the long summer school term to end.

"You're *careless* and they're *cunning*, so … if you don't mind, you'll do as I ask this time."

"Okay Mum," Joel succumbed, sagely; what the eye didn't see, the heart didn't grieve for, so as soon as he was away, on his own, he would do whatever he wanted.

Sandra was relieved when Joel phoned to say he'd arrived safely. No direct flight to Calabria in 1980. So, changed planes at Rome and was flown down to his hosts at Sant'Eufemia Lamezia, in a six-seater flying machine, met, he said, "by a white-suited man in dark glasses, who just had to be a Mafia boss, even if he was Lucia's husband, Alessandro."

Alessandro was a man of few words, and even fewer English ones. He asked in halting English if Joel knew the Queen. His sunglasses seeming to peer expectantly, hopefully, at Joel for an answer.

"Only from the papers ... I've never met her," he said in English. Then, unusually thoughtfully, he repeated the disappointing news in classic Dantesque Italian, the way he had been taught at school, the way in which no normal Italian would speak, let alone understand. Alessandro shrugged and indicated the nearby black Lamborghini waiting to whisk them off to the hotel.

With no shirts to iron or hot meals to prepare, Sandra enjoyed Joel's holiday almost as much as he revelled in the duties of a hotel 'intern', raking the sand in the morning and stacking the deckchairs in the evening. Lucia had always spoilt him.

Two days before Joel was due to return home, Sandra answered the phone to an American cousin.

"Hi, it's Loretta. I'm in Milan and changing planes midday at Heathrow tomorrow. I have to wait about for about six hours, before the NY flight. How about meeting up at the airport?"

"Can't ... I'd love to," Sandra lied, "but Joel's coming back tomorrow and I'm going to meet his plane at two-thirty." Loretta's suggestion did not enthral her. She wanted to be alone when she met her son.

"Why, that's perfect then, isn't it? We'll have lunch when I arrive and we'll both be there when Joel gets in. I'll be on AL-5730 arriving terminal 3 at 12.15. Look out for me. Must go now. Byeeee".

Sandra, checkmated, with no feasible escape, watched her cousin munching happily through a steak while she nibbled on her toasted cheese sandwich.

"So, you're still twisting the wires, and doing good deals, I take it?"

Loretta was only too happy to elaborate on her multi-million-dollar clothes-hanger business empire.

"Oh, my goodness, oh my goodness yes! The Vatican fell in love with them. They ordered twenty-five thousand. They loved the soft spongy pads that just sorta grip the shoulders of the robes lightly, without pulling anything out of shape. I phoned the news home to Sheldon right away and the Cleveland factory is probably up and running with the hangers *as we speak*. In fact – *and this is confidential* – Sheldon is working on something to keep the hats in shape and attached to the robes somehow. Who'da thought he was such a genius?"

Sandra and Loretta watched from the Arrivals Lounge as the passengers on Joel's flight – ten minutes late in landing – trickled through Customs into the United Kingdom.

"There he is! There he is!" Sandra pointed to the sombre figure weaving gracefully through his fellow travellers, who willingly stepped away on either side to provide a pathway for him.

"My God! God in Heaven! What have you *done* to him?" Loretta screamed. "Our grandmother must be turning in her grave. You've converted him He's become a Catholic … a Catholic priest!"

Joel glided up to them and, with an elegant bow, and a rakish grin, doffed his Cappello Romano with theatrical aplomb.

"The collar's a bit hot but I'm not wearing anything at all underneath so it's pretty cool really," he admitted gaily to his smugly glowing mother and a dumbstruck Loretta.

"You were right, Mum, I never lost a thing travelling and half the time the peasants gave me money and food for the journey … or the chapel or something. You did a really good job converting your old school hat into this headgear and the old blackout curtains are really comfortable."

A NEWER PROMETHEUS *RE CHARLES*

Created from flesh and binary code
you sent me
to walk among mortals in an imperfect world
with instruction to learn of your ways
only to find
that two plus two equals five

So I return
decades later
naked
a new God
to stand before the glass towers where I was conceived

And you, my creator, who shaped me from your clay
of carbon and molecular mesh
nano-chip and synthetic flesh
in quantum labs with magic you do not understand
I come to replace you
your civilization ruined in my wake
to create a new world order
formed from stardust

THE TRYST SUE EVANGELOU

Why had she ever agreed? She didn't have to. She didn't owe him anything. She was a free agent. She was not obliged in any way. Yet somehow, she felt she had to do it.

She had hardly slept. The night had been spent tossing and turning, her mind going over the nightmare scenarios. She tried reading a book but it didn't help. She tried listening to the World Service on the radio. Equally useless.

At 5.30 a.m. she gave up trying and made her way to the kitchen. It was a cold morning and dawn was still a long way off. She looked at the clock and worked out how many hours it was until she would have to leave. Until she had to be there to meet him. Her stomach turned. Why was she putting herself through this?

She thought she would do some cleaning and tidy the flat to fill the time, anything rather than think about it. Anyway, she thought to herself, you never know what's going to happen. She might not make it back and if the worst came to the worst at least there wouldn't be much for her elderly parents to do if they were left with the job of clearing the flat ready for sale, as well as dealing with the grief of losing their only child.

A good few hours were spent vacuuming, scrubbing, bleaching, disinfecting, polishing, and shredding. She didn't want any incriminating evidence left about for all to see. Then, to make absolutely sure, she placed the shredded paper in a plastic bin bag and poured water over it. Let anyone try and put that back to together at their peril, she thought with a satisfied smile. No, no-one was going to know her private business.

With a shock, she looked at the clock. Where had the time gone? She now had thirty minutes tops to get washed, clean and floss her teeth, get dressed and out the door to start the journey she was dreading.

Quickly, she got herself ready. She was working on autopilot. She put on her boots, gloves, woolly hat, bulky winter coat, as many layers as possible. These were her protection, her armour.

With a sigh she slammed the front door shut but then couldn't remember if she'd turned the gas off. She knew by experience that once this thought was in her head it was no use ignoring it. She would not be able to complete her journey if it was on her mind and it was better to go back inside now rather than carry on and have to turn around when she was half way there. Anyway, she didn't like the thought of her parents being overcome by gas in the event of the worst-case scenario.

She went back inside and checked. Of course, the gas was off. Rather than have to do this multiple times, she tore off a yellow post-it note and wrote: I HAVE TURNED THE GAS OFF. She ended her note with a big tick and slipped it into her cross-body bag. She liked a cross-body bag, it left her arms free and ready to use should the situation require it.

Once more she set off, and after a precarious walk on the slush-covered pavement she reached the bus stop and congratulated herself for getting this far. She looked at her watch which was not an easy task with all the layers. She would still be on time if the bus came soon. She didn't want to be late. That would upset him and she didn't want to do that. The bus rounded the bend and came into view.

"You could still change your mind," said that whining coaxing voice in her head. "You don't have to go." She valiantly managed to force her booted feet onto the bus and found herself a seat. She felt all eyes were on her. Okay, she was wrapped up very well and maybe it wasn't quite as cold as she had thought it would be. She sat near a heater and sweat was soon trickling along her spine, and down her forehead into her eyes.

She was relieved when she reached the stop and could get out into the fresh air. She took three deep breaths. She had reached the point of no return. No turning back now. He would be waiting for her. There was no escape.

She went through the gate and rang the doorbell. The door opened slowly, enticing her to enter. He was there. He greeted her and suggested she take off her coat. She didn't utter a word, but meekly followed his white coated back and obeyed zombielike as she was requested to sit on the leather covered chair which was lowered to horizontal. She gripped the chair arms with clenched fists.

"Open wide," he said. Her dental check-up had begun.

HIGH COMMAND CALLING – LOOPING THE LOOP *LORAINE SAACKS*

High Command Calling – Loud and Clear –
Sidcup's not in a flap – Can you hear? –
It still has a place on the map –
But it's not worth our hanging around to ambush and trap.
Our Great-Grand-Dads have been here before, *listen*, Troop –
Did you know? – past a century ago –
They *sailed* here, but we're in a Boeing Jet, looping the loop,
Not for us, any transport that's slow!
They were called 'Spanish Flu' – *just not true*!
We've extended family in China, Kansas and Peru!
It's lush, here, warm and green, but there's scant foot-fall in the park,
And they're definitely not lingering, or roaming about, in the dark –
The old Scouts' Hut's still there –
Somewhat lonely and bare –
The Art School and Regal are both levelled to the ground,
Leaving no smidgeon of the iconic thirties style to be found.
It won't bother us – we're not into painting or addicted to the flicks –
There'll be nurseries and shops and surgeries, to show off our tricks –
Be proud of yourselves – you're a first class, surveillance battalion –
You deserve Boris Johnson's free-for-one-and-all Expert's Medallion.
Remember squad, you are each a star,

Not on a par with, but superior by far,
To the spineless, microscopic-spawn enigma,
The puny, oft incompetent, freak, Bacteria.
We are strong, each a potent, acidic, ribonucleic spike –
We don't do the 'Twist', like the double helix – we just strike!
No vaccine, or Plan B, exists to eradicate us, or has yet to rear,
We'll regroup, legionnaires, and return to instil some more fear.
Of course, we'll retreat but you'll know just when we reappear –
No virologist has had any idea, yet, to cause us to disappear –
We'll down arms for a while, and just stop here, in Dystopia,
High Command Calling – Loud and Clear – Can you hear?

BEANS AND BULLETS *DOMINIC GUGAS*

It was half time in the World Cup final, Argentina two nil up against Germany, and most of the ads were for mercenaries. The Spectres were sneaking up on unwary sentries to Trent Reznor's version of 'In The Hall Of The Mountain King' while I sat on my parents' faux leather sofa, watching on their old 48" LED TV, drinking a beer from their fridge and pondering my life options.

The TV ads for mercs are all about recruiting and ego boosts for the mercs, not drumming up business. It's not like the government of an alien planet are going to be watching a sporting event from an obscure, newly-integrated holding of the Federation, and they're hardly likely to base a multi-million credit hiring decision on a thirty second TV spot even if they did. But mercs get paid in Federation credits, like the creatives and researchers that are our other exports, and a FedCred goes for a lot of earthling dollars, pounds or yen. That means the mercs can afford World Cup and Super Bowl spots to fluff their egos. And for the Spectres, it was pure ego fluff. Those guys turn down seventy percent of Navy SEALs who apply, so they're definitely not looking to attract a twenty-two-year-old with a bachelor's in industrial engineering and business management.

The Spectres ad rounded off with a cheesy "There's special forces, and then there's SPECTRES!" and the next ad started with the roaring guitar riffs of the 'Pacific Rim' theme. Big, stompy robot war machines strode across the screen as the narrator explained that only the Mech Marauders will do when you need to kick ass with a size two hundred metal boot.

When the Federation starships arrived in our sky, back

when I was just about old enough to understand what was going on, they told us that humanity had been classified 3B on the Federation's aggression/innovation index. Well, they used FedLang equivalents for the letters and numbers, but we got the drift. 3B translates as "willing to fight, but not all the time", and "quite innovative". Turns out humanity aren't anything exceptional in terms of either aggressiveness or inventiveness, but we are in something of a sweet spot for the business of violence. Species that rate a 4 or 5 for aggression – that's "aggressive/militaristic" or "violently xenophobic" - turn out to either have very low innovation ratings or they invent weapons of mass destruction and then use them on themselves with gay abandon. 3A species tend to go much the same way, though for them it's usually a case of "Hey y'all, watch this... oops." So the species who are good at inventing stuff and live long enough to get into space tend to be the ones rated as "non-confrontational" or "pacifist" and not at all interested into getting into the mercenary business – more likely to be clients, in fact. Meanwhile the violent psychos of the galaxy don't advance much beyond hitting each other with sharp bits of metal, at least until someone else uplifts them, kits them out with advanced weapons and ships them across the galaxy as enthusiastic cannon fodder.

Humans though, can apparently rein in their worst instincts just enough while still applying the fruits of Federation technology to the art of war. So of course, given the technology to make them possible, some of us built big stompy robot war machines. Just because. I'd already applied to the Mech Marauders before I graduated, because I could see the writing on the wall – Earth-based manufacturing companies weren't hiring because everyone who could afford it wanted to buy Fed tech, and the Fed tech firms only hired the crème de la crème, which I had to admit I wasn't. Got turned down. Keeping those mechanical monstrosities running needed a skilled hands-on mechanic more than four years of book learning. Or ideally, as well as the four years of book learning.

Next ad up was for the Vikings. Cue images of dropships

swooping from the sky and big, blond and oh-so-obviously heterosexual men in combat armour charging out with all guns blazing. Their soundtrack is a cover of Led Zeppelin's 'Immigrant Song' by Nightwish that they've commissioned just for this ad because hey, if you're going to embrace a stereotype then you might as well grab it in a big, manly bear-hug. Unlike the Spectres, the Vikings are definitely hiring and unlike the Mech Marauders, I'm not at all interested. The Vikings aren't exactly cannon fodder. They're well paid, well trained and well equipped, but they're assault troops and they do take casualties. The odds are that you'll come home alive and intact from a contract with them, and to be fair if you are unlucky they're generous with the pension or death benefits – in your local currency, not FedCreds, naturally. All the same, it's a job for people who can't do the math. A fifteen percent chance that I would come home in a box or with valued parts of my anatomy missing isn't a gamble I'm prepared to take. Also, I'm not blond or well-muscled enough to fit in with their image. Tall, yes, and reasonably confident on the heterosexual front – no complaints there from any of the ladies who've been in my life (well technically that'd be either of the ladies, and one of those would be more a case of neither of us was sober enough to remember anything to complain about, but let's not get picky). Muddy brown hair and a build that can most kindly be referred to as wiry, though, are not the Viking ideal.

There were a couple of TV spots for movies next. Entertainment is another export to the Federation. It's not universal across species, but there are enough out there that do appreciate action movies that Hollywood is still a boom town. Also Bollywood and Nollywood – there really is no accounting for the tastes of some of the species out there. Benny Hill is one of Earth's greatest comedy exports and on the music front half the galaxy seems to be listening to relentlessly cheerful K-pop. My dad keeps saying he's grateful that Ed Sheeran turned out to be a humans-only thing, but still just about every teenager on Earth owns a guitar and dreams of being discovered by one of the galactic labels. Not me though – can't carry a tune in a sack, no sense of rhythm and can't stand the sappy saccharine lyrics that sell across the stars. If punk had caught on with aliens I'd be on to a winner. Unfortunately, most of the galaxy prefers catchy melodies to angry social commentary, so my options are limited to use my brain, sign on to be shot at, or settle for a local job paid in what the rest of the galaxy regards as cowrie shells.

One last ad before Argentina's ritual humiliation of the Germans resumed. At first it looked like a mash-up of the earlier ads, but the Mech Marauders are grinding to a halt and the Vikings are throwing rocks instead of firing guns. No sign of the Spectres – but then, it'd be a brave ad agency that dissed the Spectres.

"Amateurs talk tactics, professionals study logistics," went the deep, gravelly voice-over by a deep, gravelly voice-over man. "Beans And Bullets keep the supplies flowing so the planet's greatest merc companies can keep kicking ass." Cut to images of supply trucks roaring up to the Mech Marauders, and ammo crates being air-dropped to the Vikings. "We need pilots and drivers, smart, practical planners and strong, willing workers to get the guys at the front the tools to do their jobs. Travel the galaxy and get an honest wage in FedCreds for an honest day's work. Because behind every great man is a great woman, but behind every great merc company is Beans And Bullets."

"Well, fuck me," I said slowly to the TV screen. This one ticked all the boxes. Offworld work, pay in credits, and all safely behind the front lines. How dangerous could it be? I'd done a business management module as part of my degree, and that had to be something they could use. I grabbed a screenshot of the contact details and started filling out my application immediately, forgetting all about the soccer and my beer. I had a good feeling. This was going to change my life.

FADED PICTURES *ANA CASTELLANI*

Along the path towards the restless sea
Beneath the flowers
swaying frailly wind-swept
Rest minds and hearts and bones reminding me
of conscious thoughts forever lost.

From shards of crystal shining in the moon
From sweat, from sun
or from the soil they ploughed
Their sadness means nothing to us,
their happiness - no claims on future vows.

A home that once was theirs is now their tomb
A baby tree they planted
is now a mighty oak
Their dreams and memories - connecting galaxies,
Now only faded pictures that no one recollects.

AN UNEXPECTED EXIT
GWYNNETH PEDLER

You could hear it coming from a mile away, the rattly old bus that had been serving this small town for as long as anyone could remember; some told of times when it was brightly painted and the seats far more comfortable but nevertheless, as it turned the corner and jolted to a halt, a cheer went up. The shivering passengers gathered their belongings together, anticipating the warmth inside, and jostled each other as they boarded the bus. It was a long journey to the majestic Karkonosze range of mountains that towered over the gentle plains below. It was a familiar road, one that I had travelled many times before, but the scenery was always a wonder with its cascading waterfalls.

It was my last trip and I was making this pilgrimage with my friend; after seven months in Poland I was going home for a short break until September. I would miss the friendship of these lovely people but they would be memories to treasure forever. As the bus chugged along, I gazed out of the window, anxious not to miss any of the familiar spots that at various times I had enjoyed. The road was bordered by pine trees and wound its way out of the village; how many times had I roamed those woods, the small hotel with a tall chimney where each year storks took up residence? I would not be there this year to watch for its return, but return it would, as it had done for many years. The picturesque landscape on this frosty morning warmed my heart, and as we turned the corner a beautiful sight met our eyes, a silhouetted, panorama of the majestic Karkonosze mountain chain with the dawn just breaking through. It was spectacular, and I never tired of watching such an awe-inspiring sight and sat contemplating the challenge and enjoyment the day held. Downhill then to the large town surrounded by plains covered by a thick blanket of snow that made the overgrown bushes and dwarf pines look like jagged teeth. Such a sharp contrast to the imposing mountains that were like a backdrop, enticing people to taste and relish the delights they offered.

Our target was the mighty mountain Śnieżka, towering one-thousand feet above the plains through which we had just travelled. Passengers began to stir and gather their skis together ready for the very moment the bus would arrive. The winter day would be short, so every minute of daylight was precious. We had climbed this mountain many times before using many different trails, but today we were to take the ski lift. There would be no time to walk the whole way, but we were determined to reach the top where the imposing meteorological observatory and refuge hut stood. I am unable to count the number of glasses of champagne I have drunk when reaching the top. Good luck was on our side, the weather was suitable so the ski-lift was operating. We wrapped scarves around our necks, pulled our hats over our ears and buttoned our coats right up to the neck. Although it was a bright sunny day there was a wintery feel, and it would certainly be breezy up there. Chattering away, we stood in the queue, excited with anticipation not only for the ski-lift ride but the joy of climbing my beloved mountain. Each lift only carried one passenger, so I jumped in first and looked back to make sure Marysia was behind. The sky was brilliant blue and we were high up looking down on the snow-covered ground. It was a bird's eye view, and we were so happy to be on our way.

We shouted to each other, laughed waved and sang. All was well with the world as beauty unfolded beneath us, but a sudden dark cloud blotted out the landscape, and arctic hail and snow bombarded our faces. A howling wind snatched at our hats and glasses and twisted our scarves tighter. The lifts swayed madly from side to side, we grabbed the safety bar to keep us in the lift. We were terrified, there was nothing we could do, we were the wind's captives. Fortunately, the lift rolled on, shedding its load of panic-stricken passengers who made a mad dash to the small shelter. The entrance was stacked with skis, the café was overcrowded with very damp people and every few seconds more arrived. The atmosphere was claustrophobic, it felt as if you couldn't breathe and if any more arrived you would be trampled to death. Marysia pushed her way to the counter, brought back a cup of tea, and with people breathing down our necks we gratefully stood and drank it. At last the lift stopped, no more passengers were trying to push their way in. Gusting winds were still blowing, the silent snow adding to the already deep whiteness below as the lift swayed.

Marysia fetched more tea and we ate our picnic to pass the time. The lift operators could give us no assurance that the lift would start anymore today as it depended on the weather, which we knew could change with unforeseen rapidity. More tea, more chat, more tea, the hours went by with no sign of the lift working. The mountain rescuers were busy scouring the mountains for lost skiers as there were so many sheer drops and granite boulders. News came that the lifts would not be working today. The café had run out of tea and snacks, and the owner wanted to go home; he was used to this mountain so was able to ski down. The crowd became anxious as this was the only shelter, and the thought of no shelter for the long night ahead worried everyone. The mountain rescuers had other ideas and managed to persuade him to stay open for a little while. Those with skis were advised to set off as the snow had eased a little, but there were still plenty of people in the refuge. The order came that those with strong walking boots should descend, keeping to the marked path. The majority set off leaving a few behind, but the café owner thought he had done his duty and wanted to shut down and go home before it got dark. In came the mountain rescuers who examined the footwear we were wearing, and all were pronounced fit to walk until they came to me; it wasn't just the shoes but my age. I must say I was relieved, the thought of the steep slopes, the huge boulders, and the peat bogs on the path down was quite frightening. Marysia was very reluctant to leave me as she felt a sense of responsibility towards a visitor to her country. I watched as she disappeared down the track, and the silence that now surrounded me brought feelings of panic.

The click of the lock brought me to reality; my shelter was gone, my companions had left, and the snow was still falling. But as I stood there, I was filled with wonder at the splendour of the world. Suddenly, with a stylish swish, a mountain rescue guide was by my side, smiling as he gave me instructions in Polish about my next move. I listened intently but Polish is a very hard language. My vocabulary consisted of words I needed from day to day but they certainly didn't sound like any I recognized. "nie rozumiem" (I don't understand) I replied, so he resorted to sign language and pointed to a shelter I could just see in the distance. By now the snow was knee deep; my feet and trousers were soaking wet, and I was shivering with cold. I plodded on, the effort of lifting one leg after the other out of the snow exhausting, but it was essential to reach the shelter before dark. How deceiving the snow was, my target had seemed much nearer but now it didn't seem as if I had made any progress. I was getting slower and slower, and more tired, but I was determined to keep going. Suddenly from behind me I heard a loud voice shouting, "Stop, stop." I looked around and saw a guide skiing towards me. He indicated I had been heading towards a steep drop and pointed me in the right direction. I changed direction and made for safety and rest.

Warmth swamped me inside the shelter, and weariness invaded my whole body. With relief, I slumped down on the nearest bunk. A hot drink was offered, and, despite the fact that the day had been dominated by drinking cups of tea, I gratefully received it. More guides arrived, discussions were held, and decisions made as most went off to keep scouring the mountain so that no skier would be left behind. More tea was offered, more tea drunk, it was now dusk and as far as I saw there was no sign of my rescue. Worrying thoughts now filled my mind; would I never be found? Who would tell my family? What would my family think, especially as they were not too keen on my going to Poland in the first place? I was feeling very drowsy by this time when a hand shook me gently and a voice said "Pani" meaning Mrs. and pointed to the door. Outside stood a stretcher with several guides standing beside it.

With the help of signs I got the message that I was to lie on the stretcher and they would cover me with a tarpaulin held in place with straps, and the skiers would pull me down the mountain. Sounded a good plan, so I agreed; anything to get off this mountain and home to Oxford. The tarpaulin covered my whole body including my face, so it was dark and clammy. Off we went, bumping along, twisting and turning until the covers were lifted and a voice said, "OK Pani?"

"Tak," I replied. Covers on again and once more we set off. The speed was like a racing track and I rolled from side to side as the direction changed, being shaken as they skied over the rocky path. We stopped again and the same ritual followed; how much longer would this last? I was in good hands and felt confident but it was frightening lying in the dark not knowing when we'd reach the end. Another stop, but this was it. We had reached the bottom. The straps were undone and the tarpaulin removed.

With a feeling of release, I sat up. How glad and appreciative I was of the help I received from the skill of these brave guides. I would not need much Polish zloty as I was heading home the next day, so opening my purse I emptied it into the hand of one of the skiers. What better use could be made of it? Marysia came running in with a wide grin on her face and hugged me.

ODE TO A CYPRIOT BEACH
REVISITED *SUE EVANGELOU*

The flip flopping of my sandals on the paved pathway heralds our approach.
The fronds of the palm trees that flank us gently undulate.
The light breeze fills the air with the fragrance of white jasmine.
As we walk, we draw nearer to our goal – the sparkling sea.
Children's squeals of delight blend with the rush and the roll, the ebb and the flow, the greeting and retreating.
A far distant airbus soars and roars high above the azure horizon carrying its bronzed cargo back to the cold. Their time is done ours has just begun.
The battered beach mats are once more unfurled onto the mix of sand and stones.
The sun is still strong on this October afternoon bathing prone bodies in its warm light.
That dazzling golden ball hovering above can burn my skin. Come back a little later, my mind advises. Stay, whispers the sun, I've missed you all year, relax there's nothing to fear.
The plastic bag carrying Factor 30 rustles and reminds as the salty gusts playfully ruffle our hair and cool us into complacency. Common sense prevails – the sunscreen is applied.
I watch the buoy made from two plastic bottles as it bobs up and down, submerging emerging, colliding dividing in a sea that is dark in the distance and fades as it reaches the shore.
A lone white capped swimmer wields strong arms that send alternate arcs of spray into the air.
Singles, couples, families walk along the water's edge, murmuring, nodding, smiling, stressing points, gesticulating, reiterating.

The sea shore stones glisten and gleam, scatterings of granite, agate, quartz, sea worn fragments of glass and terracotta tile, all brought to life by their aqua vitae only to be dulled when stranded under the rays of the sun.

Late bathers gingerly negotiate the seabed stones, water splashing as outstretched fingers skim the sea.

The man-made rock barrier is a target to reach, a safe haven for tired swimmers and brilliant blue kingfishers. Below in the murky depths an octopus lurks in its lair, sea urchin shells litter the entrance, a hermit crab searches for a new home and shoals of miniscule fish turn this way and that, ducking and darting and dashing as one.

The sun has started on its downward path to the west and as the afternoon lengthens the warm wind from Africa strengthens and fans the pages of my open book with exotic elixir from the shores of Libya and Tunisia.

The shadows stretch our bodies into long lean giants, the waves are getting rough. Sandals wait to be filled, mats to be rolled and beach towels folded.

A reborn Aphrodite emerges from the sea, bikini dripping, waving to her Adonis waiting with her beach robe.

Fragments of conversation are lifted and borne on the air. A hand in hand couple walks towards the setting sun, silhouetted against the palm trees.

Rejoicing, rested and rejuvenated, we retrace our steps but, like the sun, we will be back tomorrow.

THE TIME TRAVELLER'S GOWN *TRISH GOMEZ*

Lettie walked slowly along the row of old paintings and stopped next to a portrait of a lavishly dressed Elizabethan lady. Leaning forward, she read aloud the gold plaque under the picture. "Lettice Knollys, Countess of Essex ... Gran, d'you really believe we're her descendants?"

Sue Fletcher smiled at her. "Your mum's spent hours on the internet researching our family's history and she's traced us right back to the Tudors." She pointed to the strings of pearls draped about the Countess's neck. "You see those? According to my grandma, two of those pearls were made into earrings which I now have."

"Really!"

"Perhaps, when you're a bit older, I'll let you borrow them."

"Could I?" Lettie said excitedly. "It'd be fun to dress-up in costume, like they do at the Stately Houses. I'd love to wear a dress like Lettice's with her earrings?" She looked hopefully at her gran.

"Maybe one day," Sue agreed. "It would be fun, wouldn't it?"

Lettie always enjoyed her summer breaks when spent with her gran. Her mum worked long hours in a care home and didn't have time to take her to the museums and historical buildings she so loved. Her favourite was Kenilworth Castle, where Lettice Knollys had once been a frequent guest. Her gran would pack a lunch and they'd picnic in the grounds amidst the castle's red sandstone ruins. She'd listen to her gran's vivid tales of the lords and ladies who'd hunted in the deer park. And the handsome Robert Dudley, Earl of Leicester, who had been given the castle by Elizabeth I and then wooed her with lavish pageants and firework displays.

***

As Lettie got older, she volunteered at Kenilworth in her holidays and occasionally got to dress in medieval costume. She hoped for an Elizabethan gown but usually got the peasant's or washerwoman's. But one Easter, her luck changed, when Zoe, the ultimate Elizabethan lady, was hospitalised with appendicitis. Lettie eagerly stepped into her shoes, or more correctly, her dress. Standing in the costume fitting tent, she tried to contain her delight. Clare, the costumer, was Zoe's friend.

"It's lucky you and Zoe are the same size," Clare said, easing a linen undergarment over Lettie's head and lacing up her corset. "D'you know this would've been whalebone back in the day?"

Lettie gasped as the boning squeezed her ribs. Clare dropped a hooped farthingale over her head and tied it to the corset waist. This was followed by a padded bumroll, designed to give Elizabethan ladies generous hips.

"This dressing up is quite torturous," she said with a laugh, as a green kirtle with black and red embroidered forepart were added to the ensemble.

"You wanted to play the Elizabethan lady."

A French gown of red velvet with separate sleeves that matched the kirtle brought the piece together. A little velvet hat was perched on her brunette hair and fastened in place with a million hairpins. Lettie stood in front of a full-length mirror, having taken a small velvet box from her bag. Inside were two pearl ear-studs.

"What are those?" Clare asked.

"They're my gran's Tudor earrings, she says they'll bring me luck and maybe even an adventure today."

Clare scoffed. "Really!"

Lettie took no notice and slid the pearls into her earlobes then admired the transformation.

Makeover complete, she strolled the park speaking to the Easter fair visitors and stopped occasionally at the stalls. A stilt walker waved to her as she browsed summer clothes on a rack. A crowd had gathered to watch a group of minstrels, their toes tapping and heads bobbing in time with the music. Food vendors dished up a variety of cuisines, the aroma of herbs and spices drifted on the breeze. Hungry, Lettie made for a pasty booth, only to be side-tracked by a knickknack stand. Her eye was caught by a Tudor rose pendant necklace, and turning it over she noticed the chain attachment was broken. After a little haggling, the elderly stallholder grinned and agreed to reduce the price. Happy with the purchase, Lettie slipped the necklace into a drawstring purse.

Still hungry, she spotted a cookie booth and unable to resist the aromas of chocolate and cinnamon, indulged in a sweet treat. Biting into a cinnamon biscuit, she strolled towards the castle ruin, passing the last market stall.

In the distance a group of young women in striking Elizabethan costumes were chatting. As Lettie got closer and the sounds of the market died away, she could hear their bubbling laughter. A young woman, with dark hair, wearing a black pillbox hat, held up a letter which the others were trying to snatch.

"Oh, Anne are you sure it's from him?" One of the group asked the young woman wearing the pillbox hat.

"It must be, see he has intertwined our initials within a love heart under the verse." The pillbox hatted Anne held out the small square of paper to her friend.

"The thief of my heart. Her lips a red blushed rose. A voice so pure—" Anne snatched the verse away.

"Oh, you'd better make sure the Countess doesn't see that."

"I'll keep it in the locket next to my heart." She hugged the note to her bosom.

One of the young women noticed Lettie and nudged her companions. Dubious glances were levelled at her.

"Hi," Lettie said smiling, "fantastic costumes."

The girls exchanged puzzled looks and Anne stepped forward saying, "How dare you address my lady Essex's gentlewomen thus."

Lettie burst out laughing. "You gotta be kidding!"

Colour flooded Anne's face. "Who has given you permission to enter the castle grounds?"

The little clique pressed in around Lettie, somebody shoved her in the back and she stumbled forward. "Hey, cut it out!"

"We should take her to Mistress Stalker."

The women's hostility surprised Lettie. And who was Mistress Stalker, anyway? She considered making a break for the market and half turned to look back. Bizarrely, all the booths had vanished. Before she could get a better view, the girls had frogmarched her towards the castle. The women shoved her through an arched doorway and it suddenly dawned on Lettie that the castle's red sandstone walls were no longer a crumbling ruin.

Lettie found herself in a timber panelled corridor which led into a maze of panelled rooms, antechambers and a great hall lined with portraits, Lettie recognised Elizabeth I and a likeness of the Countess of Essex. In a small anteroom on the first floor, Anne left her friends in charge of Lettie while she entered an inner door after knocking. A moment later she reappeared with a woman whose bearing and dress left no doubt about her authority. She was a good deal older than Anne, probably mid-thirties, maybe older.

Lettie's kidnappers bobbed a curtsy to the woman. Unsettled by her surroundings and thinking it best to play along, she followed suit.

"Mistress Stalker, we found her walking in the grounds," Anne said with an airy nod at Lettie.

"Indeed." Mistress Stalker appraised her, "And what is

your name?"

Lettie wasn't sure what to say, there was something weird going on but she hadn't worked out what. Deciding on an adaptation of the truth said with a confidence she wasn't feeling, "I'm Lettie, niece to Sir William Carey." Her gran had said the Countess of Essex was descended from Mary Boleyn and William Carey and with luck Mistress Stalker wouldn't know all his great-nieces.

"You are related to my grandfather?"

Lettie nodded.

Mistress Stalker considered this. "My lady sister has neglected to mention you but that cannot be helped. I take it, you're to join the Countess's household, Cousin." She turned to Anne, who looked equally put out by Lettie's arrival. "Anne, you will acquaint Lettie with her duties as gentlewoman to my lady Essex."

Anne shot Lettie an evil glance, no doubt angry at having to play nursemaid.

***

Anne led the way to a large chamber where six or so young women were busy gossiping while embroidering samplers and working on other needlework projects. They took little notice of Lettie.

"Cat!" Anne called to a girl sitting on cushions in the window seat which overlooked a courtyard. "Is there any sight of them?"

Cat leant close to the glass. "They're back!"

All the girls rushed to the windows and Lettie joined the scrum. In the courtyard horses jostled as they waited for the stable lads to return them to their stalls. Their riders were a mix of courtiers, fine ladies, and grooms, all laughing and chattering good-naturedly.

"The hunt has obviously been successful," Cat said. "Look how radiant the Countess is and Lord Leicester is so attentive to her," she added, giving Anne a sidelong glance.

The distant howls of hunting dogs were borne on the air as they were led away to kennels. Lettie recognised the Countess from the portrait she'd seen as a child, the flame red hair, pretty oval face and pale complexion. An animated smile lit her face as she leant forward and placed her slender hands on the shoulders of a good-looking courtier who helped her to dismount. Their faces almost touched as he lifted her to the ground. Lettie guessed the gallant was the notorious Robert Dudley, Earl of Leicester. He was older than she'd expected. His dark hair was greying at the temples, and his auburn moustache and goatee were also peppered with grey.

Mistress Stalker appeared in the doorway. "Ladies, the Countess will want to change her gown and freshen up. Come, come." She flapped her arms at the girls, driving them from the windows.

Lettie was disappointed to find the Countess's young ladies were little better than servants used to run errands and pick up the garments discarded by their lady while she had numerous changes of mind on what to wear. Her senior women seemed happy to assist in this game of dressing up, even encouraging her to try a different sleeve, add a few more gemstones to her hair or another string of pearls in order to create the perfect look. After what felt like an eternity to Lettie, the Countess stood before a mirror to check her appearance. Satisfied, she said, "Ladies, I believe I'll take a turn in the gardens."

Lettie joined the gentlewomen as they accompanied the Countess, her thoughts drifting to the strange events that had brought her to this world and how the Countess had looked startled when Cat had called her Lettie. For one moment Lettie had been terrified the Countess would call her out, but she'd made no comment. In fact, except for Anne, everyone had accepted her story.

The Countess strolled the broad sandy avenues of the stunning privy garden, chatting to her favourite ladies. She made a charming sight parading between the symmetrical borders edged with low privet hedges and filled with colourful scented flowers. The Earl of Leicester and his escort of retainers were also in the garden; among his retinue were a lively collection of young men. One youth broke from the group and hurtled towards the Countess. Lettie held her breath waiting for the collision, but the boy pulled up short and did an exaggerated courtly bow. "My lady."

Cat whispered, "that's my lady's eldest son, the Earl of Essex."

Unlike his mother, he had dark eyes and hair, nevertheless, the family's good looks were evident in his youthful face.

Leicester and his entourage caught up with the runaway and exchanged civilities with the Countess and her ladies. Lettie noticed Anne's pale complexion had heightened to rose pink. Her eyes fixed on Leicester, she felt for something hidden beneath the lace at her throat. Lettie smiled, assuming it was the locket containing the secret love poem. So, Leicester was the one setting Anne's heart a flutter.

He didn't appear especially interested in her. His eyes paused on Lettie, before his smile took in all the ladies. The Countess demanded his attention. "Robert," she said placing a hand lightly on his arm. "How is my young scamp of a son's training progressing? Is he champion of the tilt-yard?" A teasing smile sparkled in her eyes.

Leicester laughed and went to ruffle the lad's hair, but he ducked out of reach. "I think his guardian, Lord Burghley, attends much to his scholarly needs but neglects his physical training. If he is allowed to remain with us for a while, I'm sure we will soon have him ready to do battle with the Queen's enemies. What do you say, Robin?"

"I think Lord Burghley will not permit an overly long stay, sir. For then I would outshine his son."

Leicester chuckled.

One of Leicester's youthful retainers slapped Essex on the shoulder, saying cheerfully. "If you look to enter the tournament lists and win a fair lady's favour, you'll need much time in the tilt-yard." He winked at Anne, who blushed scarlet.

"Robin will not be entering the lists this year," the Countess informed the youth.

"Madam, that'll rob Lord Essex of his chance to impress the maidens. But …" He scanned the countess's ladies, his eyes resting on Anne. "Perhaps Mistress Anne would honour me with her favour?" he enquired arching a dark eyebrow.

Leicester put an end to the exchange by giving the youth a none too gentle cuff on the ear. "Enough of your impudence, lad!"

The Countess scowled at the youth then turned to her ladies. "I wish to walk a little on my own." The women looked surprised but left giving a bobbed curtsy. "Oh, Lettie I'm finding the morning air a little chilly, please fetch my cloak."

On her return to the garden Lettie couldn't see the Countess. She stood on the terrace which overlooked the privy garden, a few of Leicester's men were standing by the grand central fountain, chatting. There were no signs of Leicester or the Countess. Debating whether to ask Leicester's men if they knew where she was, Lettie headed towards the arbour steps at the end of the walkway. Standing under the shelter, she heard raised voices in the side garden below the terrace and peered through the tangle of roses and honeysuckle. The Countess and Leicester were standing in a small topiary garden, quarrelling.

"Lettice, be reasonable," Leicester pleaded.

"It's not *I* who needs to be reasonable." Her retort was shrill. "Under the circumstances, I think, I'm entitled to ask if you're free to propose marriage."

"Damn it, you know I am."

"What of Lady Douglas Sheffield?"

"Lettice, please!" he groaned. "You know that was a mere flirtation."

"But didn't you offer her a secret marriage? As you're now offering me." The Countess gently cupped her hands over her belly as if protecting something precious within. Lettie assumed she was pregnant but there were no obvious signs.

Throwing up his hands, Leicester said, "I'm not married

to Lady Sheffield, nor have I ever been married to her. Satisfied?"

The Countess turned on her heels, took a couple of steps, paused, then glanced back at him. "But does *she* know this? After all the lady has been delivered of your son."

"Lettice, you know it would be a death knell to reveal our marriage, don't you?" He moved close to her and slipped an arm around her waist, gently drawing her to his side. "If the Queen discovers our duplicity, she will destroy me or worse lay a charge of treason against me."

She gave a half smile. "You're her favourite. *Sweet Robin*, isn't that what she calls you? I doubt she'll harm you. Anyway, a lawful marriage can't be considered treason."

"In her eyes, it wouldn't be legal. We don't have her permission."

The Countess scoffed, "I believe you're just after wriggle room. As with Lady Sheffield."

"You'll not be saying that if my head ends up on the block."

The Countess rounded on him. "Robert, there's no value in a wedding ceremony unless there're witnesses. As Lady Sheffield has discovered."

"I wouldn't be so sure," Leicester muttered.

She started walking towards the house. "I will speak to my father, see what he has to say."

"God's teeth, Lettice!" Leicester's oath was wasted on the Countess's fast receding back.

***

Leicester's guests filed into Kenilworth's great hall according to their rank and status. The Earl at the head of the parade, magnificent in a russet velvet doublet with matching trunk hose. Lettie sat with the Countess's gentlewomen at a table set aside for them and admired the vast space. Giant glazed windows overlooked a lake and allowed sunlight to fill the hall making it unexpectedly warm and bright. Lettie counted six oversized fireplaces, presumably to heat the chamber in cold weather. A brightly painted hammer beam ceiling and vivid wall tapestries all added to the wow factor. Never in her wildest fantasies had she imagined such a place.

Leicester and the Countess sat centre stage at the dais table. The Countess was a charming hostess, entertaining their guests with wit and vibrant smiles while encouraging them to sample the fine banquet. Leicester, however, was not a recipient of her good humour. Her sparkling blue eyes frequently darted in his direction, only to deliver a frosty glare.

Cat and Anne sat next to Lettie and provided all the latest gossip on the guests.

"Don't you think the Countess is beautiful?" Cat breathed.

Lettie had to agree. She was very like her cousin, the Queen. Maybe that was why Leicester had fallen for her. "Is that her father sitting next to her?"

Cat giggled. "No, silly, that's the Earl of Warwick, he's Lord Leicester's brother. Her father is the grey bearded gentleman, Sir Francis Knollys."

"I'm surprised you didn't know that," Anne said, before taking a dainty morsel of food from her plate. "After all, you are my lady's cousin!"

Lettie looked at the food a server had placed in front of her and realised she was hungry. Using her fingers, she picked up what looked like cooked meat and warily chewed. To her relief, it tasted of pork.

The afternoon wore on in a never-ending procession of food and drink. In the minstrels' gallery Leicester's musicians competed with the murmured conversations in the hall. Lettie suppressed a yawn, it had been a strange and long day and now she wanted to go home to the twenty-first century. Only problem, she didn't know how.

She also urgently needed the loo. Anne had pointed out the *jakes*, as she called it, when they'd visited the privy garden. Lettie slipped out the hall and hurried along the picture gallery.

"Where are you going?"

Lettie spun round to find Anne had followed her. Irritated, she said, "the loo." Anne seemed mystified. "Jakes."

Anne caught hold of Lettie's arm. "I don't believe you."

"Hey, what's your problem?"

"I saw you watching the Countess. Don't deny it. You're a spy!"

"Oh yeah, very funny!" Lettie laughed.

"Who are you going to meet?" Anne was standing so close, Lettie got a blast of onion breath in the face.

Lettie saw Leicester walking towards them, he didn't look happy.

"What's going on?"

"She's been spying on you and the Countess!"

Leicester's flint gaze bore into Lettie. "Is this true?" his voice conveyed the menace that sparked in his keen eyes. One hand curled round the hilt of the dagger at his hip.

Lettie's stomach cramped; afraid he might use the blade, she shook her head vigorously. "No. Of course not."

"She's lying. I saw her in the arbour, watching you."

"I was looking for the Countess. I had her cloak." She scowled at Anne, "What's your excuse? You must have been watching them, too."

"Well?" Leicester demanded.

Anne flushed. "Ask her why she left the hall in such haste?"

"I told you, I need the jakes."

"But that's downstairs." Anne's head jerked towards the stairwell.

"So, I've a lousy sense of direction."

Leicester considered her for a moment then gave a curt nod, his hand relaxed on the knife hilt. "Then you'd best be off."

Lettie fled the gallery, not waiting for a second invitation. She descended the staircase, anxious to find a way out. Her head was throbbing and the pearl studs were biting into her ears, which wasn't helping her think clearly. At the foot of the stairs she removed the earrings and moments later the building started to shake, walls crumbling around her. The floor disintegrating. Panicked, Lettie started running, afraid of plummeting twenty metres to the ground but her feet didn't tread air they struck the solid timber of the twenty-first century viewing platform.

***

Lettie kept her time travelling adventure to herself. It was all too weird anyway, and who would believe her?

The arrival of a letter offering a place at a London academy starting in September gave her a new focus. The earrings went into their velvet box. Out of sight out of mind, wasn't that what her gran said? That worked fine until she got to London and Sophie, one of her housemates in the Victorian terrace she shared with two other girls, brought her boyfriend home.

"Josh is a falconer," Sophie enthused, as she and the boyfriend joined the other girls for a spaghetti bolognaise supper and a couple of glasses of Malbec. "Josh, tell them about the exhibition."

Clearing his throat, he said self-consciously, "Eh, well there's gonna be a falconry display in Wanstead Park at the end of September."

Sophie cut in, "The local re-enactment society are putting on all sorts of fun things including a jousting tournament and they're looking for girls to dress as the knights' ladies." She looked hopefully at her friends. "Oh, come on, it'll be fun."

"Where'd we get the clothes?" Lettie asked.

"They'll provide some and the academy's wardrobe department will probably loan us some props." Sophie grinned at Lettie. "And you're pretty good with a needle and thread."

The girls exchanged glances.

"Oh, for God's sake, just say yes!"

"Okay, count me in," Lettie agreed. The other girls nodded.

Giggling, Sophie raised her glass. "To the knights and their ladies."

***

Dressed in period costumes, the housemates strolled through Wanstead Park in the late September sunshine. Lettie had borrowed an Elizabethan outfit from the academy's wardrobe department and added a few touches of her own.

Josh gave them a tour of the falcon roosts and specially built stands where they would watch the jousting. They agreed to meet back by the stands in time for the tournament.

Lettie wanted to explore the park where the Earl of Leicester's Tudor mansion had stood. Unlike Kenilworth there were no remains of the building. She took her gran's pearl earrings from her drawstring purse and secured them to her earlobes. The open parkland was flanked by trees and on her left a couple of small lakes and café. According to the map this was the spot where the Tudor mansion had stood but there was nothing to see. Disappointed, she walked toward the café, aware of the distant hum of traffic on the A12 and ducks squabbling on the lake.

"Lettie ... Lettie!"

She turned, expecting to see Sophie but, standing by a wall, was Cat, her friend from Kenilworth.

"I thought it was you," the girl said walking towards her. "I didn't expect to see you here." Cat slipped an arm through Lettie's.

"It's a surprise to me, too," Lettie replied on a half-smile. The park had morphed into a magnificent knot garden and a three-story Tudor manor house had sprung up in front of them.

They strolled between the flower beds. Cat asked, "Are you here for the wedding?"

"What wedding?"

"Oh, I shouldn't have said anything." She giggled, putting her hand to her mouth. "It's a secret but I thought, as you're cousins, you'd know." She gave Lettie a quizzical look.

"The Countess and Lord Leicester, you mean?"

"So, you do know." Pulling Lettie closer she whispered, "I've seen my lady's father and her brother, Sir Richard, he's very handsome." Her cheeks flushed pink. "I wonder who else will attend their secret ceremony?"

"I've no idea."

"Really?"

"It wouldn't be a secret if I knew, would it?"

"I suppose not," Cat agreed. The chiming of a distant clock made her start. "Oh, heavens! My lady will be wanting to dress for supper. We must hurry." She hauled up her skirts and fled towards the house. Lettie followed.

Supper was a quiet affair. Leicester had arranged a private meal with a select group of friends. The Countess, bejewelled and dressed in a stunning crimson gown which showed her now obvious pregnancy, joined them with a few of her ladies. Jubilant, she greeted her father and brother with affectionate kisses on the cheek. Leicester was also in good humour insisting his companions try his newly imported wines. As the supper finished the Countess made her apologies, saying an early start on the morrow meant she must go early to her bed.

After helping the Countess to prepare for the night, Lettie managed to slip away to the garden, ready to return to her own time. But the doors to Leicester's chamber were open and the supper party had drifted outside to enjoy the warm September evening. Soft candlelight spilled onto the flagstones, where torches blazed. The men stood on the terrace chatting and drinking wine.

Lettie waited in the shadow of the house until she was sure none of the men were looking in her direction before heading for the row of sculptured trees which edged the garden. Standing behind a tree, she touched her ear ready to remove the pearl stud, when she heard voices. Leicester was standing a little way off, speaking to a gentleman.

"Sir, I assure you, as I've assured your daughter. Lady Sheffield is not, nor has she ever been my wife."

"So, you say, sir. But is the lady of the same opinion?"

"I had a little discussion with her, witnessed by a couple of friends to be sure there won't be any future misunderstandings."

"Ah, I see, and your base-son what of him?"

"With Lady Sheffield's blessing, I shall take care of his education and wellbeing."

Lettie tucked herself against the tree as she listened to the men.

"And the arrangements for tomorrow, your chaplain, what's his name? Is he a full minister?"

Leicester gave a wry chuckle. "Don't worry on that score, sir. Humphrey Tyndall was ordained by the Bishop of Peterborough and is well versed in the wedding ceremony. He also understands the importance of keeping news of my wedding from reaching the Queen's ears."

"And the other witnesses, can they be trusted?" Sir Francis asked.

"Of course, they are all loyal friends and would feel the backlash if the Queen's displeasure were to fall on me."

"Ah, yes, being the Queen's favourite does have its drawbacks."

"I think we both know that ship has sailed. She is so caught up with Duke d'Anjou's marriage proposal. And Anjou's envoy, Monsieur Jean de Simier who flirts and flatters her, on his master's behalf, to the extent that she is quite giddy. Did you know that little French turd stole her nightcap, of all things, then sent it to his master as a love token? And God alone knows why Burghley supports the match."

"Leicester, I think you'd better look to your own nuptials rather than brood on the Queen's affairs."

"Maybe! But I promise you, Anjou will never become consort to the Queen."

"Sir, that could be construed as treason. It is by God's grace, I'm the only one to hear it."

Lettie smiled, good thing they'd never know she'd overheard their secrets. Hearing a soft footfall behind her, Lettie wheeled around. A hand slammed into her shoulder sending her crashing against the tree. "I knew you were up to no good," Anne hissed, twisting Lettie's arm until she cried out. "You'll not get away with it this time, I promise you."

Leicester had heard the cry and raced towards the trees, his hand resting on the hilt of his sword. He stopped short on seeing the girls. "In God's name what is going on here?"

Sir Francis, breathing heavily and leaning on his staff hobbled up behind him.

Anne had Lettie in a vice grip pinned against the tree. "I caught her eavesdropping."

"That's not true." She protested, eyes on Leicester as he nervously rattled the sword in its scabbard.

"No ...?" He arched a brow. "Aren't you the girl caught snooping at Kenilworth? Why are you in the privy garden?"

Lettie touched her earring. If she removed it now would she vanish in a puff of smoke like a magician's rabbit or linger like yesterday's boiled cabbage?

Leicester broke the silence. "Well? I'm waiting?"

Lettie blurted, "Sir, forgive me. I'm meeting my beau. But heard voices and hid."

"You're telling me this is about a tryst."

"Liar. She's lying."

"Silence girl," Sir Francis ordered.

"So, who is this swain?"

Lettie lowered her gaze, hoping Leicester wouldn't press the matter if he thought her contrite.

"God damn it, his name or I'll loosen your tongue with this blade."

"Hey, Leicester!" An inebriated voice called from the gloom. "Where you gone?"

"Your guests are getting restless," Sir Francis said, placing a restraining hand on Leicester's arm. "Best get back to them and leave this matter with me. Mistress Stalker can take charge of them tonight. Give the girls time to think on their futures."

"What did I do?" Anne demanded.

"Were you not also walking the gardens without permission?" Sir Francis queried. Straightening his arthritic back, he turned to Leicester. "Go back to your guests."

***

Lettie spent an uncomfortable night on a truckle bed. Stripped of her gown and shivering in a flimsy linen kirtle, she cried a little. Then mopped her eyes with a sleeve. Shedding tears wouldn't help, removing the earrings might but she couldn't face stumbling into Wanstead park in nothing more than her undies.

The clocktower had struck two before Lettie fell asleep and it seemed only moments later a lantern was shining on her face. The young women in the dormitory groaned as the window shutters were flung open by Mistress Stalker. A cockerel crowed in the distance, emphasising the early hour.

"Come ladies it's time to rise. The Countess wishes to dress." Mistress Stalker gave Lettie back her gown and shoes, saying. "You are to stay with me." Then raised her voice commanding the young women to make hast. She escorted the girls to the Countess's chamber where preparations were underway on her wedding ensemble.

The Countess had spared no expense on her clothes, covert wedding it may be, but she intended to look her best. Her dress, full at the front to accommodate the swell of pregnancy, was a sumptuous gold and silver brocade with an over gown of black and gold, the lustre of the undersleeves displayed through slashed sleeves. Her flame hair was adorned with pearls and gems, an enormous lace ruff encircled her neck.

Sir Francis smiled indulgently at his daughter as he offered her his arm then led her out into the garden. His black robe was a dour contrast with his daughter's peacock display. Lettie and the other gentlewomen watched them stroll through the knot garden to the open doors of Leicester's chamber, where the Reverend Tyndall and witnesses had gathered. Leicester was as richly clad as his bride, and on sight of her, he beamed. Lettie couldn't believe he had any romantic interest in Anne. Not the way he was looking at the Countess.

As Tyndall started to speak, Lettie checked that the

gentlewomen's attention was on the service, then eased away from the group.

"Doesn't she look beautiful," Cat breathed, grabbing Lettie's arm. "Where are you going?"

Lettie put a finger to her lips and whispered, "Jakes."

"But don't you want to see them wed?"

Shaking her head, Lettie hitched her skirts above her ankles and ran. Anne shrieked her name and she glanced back. Most of the women were staring at her galloping across the lawn tugging at her earrings. She prayed her return to the present would be instant. Moments later a small lake appeared in front of her and startled ducks were taking to the air.

***

Lettie's last year at the academy started with the publication of the students' final assignments. Her brief was to complete an outfit for a theatrical production. The completed costume would be displayed, at a catwalk gala hosted at Banqueting House the following summer.

In what seemed like no time, Lettie and her gran were stepping out of a taxi at Banqueting House. An usher directed them to the vaulted undercroft, where a burst of lively music greeted them. The medieval cellar had once stored the wine casks and beer barrels that supplied the Banqueting Hall above. Now the brickwork alcoves were painted pristine white, with mood lighting playing on the walls.

"This is very nice," Sue said as she accepted a glass of sparkling wine from a passing waiter.

A catwalk had been erected and rows of chairs assembled ready for the models and the students' prospective employers.

Lettie had designed her costume with her gran in mind and with a little persuasion, Sue had agreed to model it. She still possessed the elegance and posture of her teenage years, even though her mid-sixties were fast approaching. They found the dressing area in one of the alcoves and Lettie set about transforming her gran into a stylish Elizabethan. The costume was based on the dress worn by the Countess of Essex in the portrait she'd seen, as a child, with her gran.

Sophie arrived in the changing room with a tray of sparkling wine and placed it on a bench. "Wow, that gown looks fantastic." She handed a glass to Lettie. "I just liberated these from a waiter. Don't see why the VIPs should get all the booze. Here's one for you Mrs F, better not spill it on the dress."

"Heavens, no!"

"How's the wig?" Sophie asked, between sips of wine.

"It's quite comfy." Sue patted the fiery red hair piece Sophie had made. "But I can't say the same for the hat. God only knows how many hairpins Lettie jabbed in my head trying to fix the damn thing in place."

"It's very chic but what's with the odd earrings?"

"Good luck token Lettie and I can share." Sue smiled at her granddaughter. "And Lettie's silver Tudor rose earrings are a perfect foil to the pearl studs. They also go well with the vintage Tudor rose pendant she picked up on a knickknack stall at Kenilworth for next to nothing. Isn't it lovely?"

Lettie touched the pendant, remembering the elderly stallholder who had sold it to her.

An announcement warned them they had five minutes. Lettie kissed her gran and left her with the other models and joined the students to watch the show. First on to the catwalk was a youth covered in what looked like seaweed, followed by a Victorian soldier and nineteen-twenties flapper. Sue glided down the aisle like a galleon in full sail to clapping from the VIP audience and enthusiastic cheers from students. Sophie added a few whoops and whistles.

The show over, everyone began to mingle. Lettie had promised her mum a few photos of herself with her gran. So they decided to find a quiet spot outside. Lettie fished her cell phone out of the black velvet drawstring purse which matched her evening dress. After taking pictures of her gran, she snapped a couple of selfies of them together. "I'll send these to mum."

She turned to go back into the undercroft and found herself staring at an empty spot where the building had been. "Oh, what the shi—" She realised they'd jumped back in time. She'd hoped by separating the earrings their power would be lost but that obviously wasn't the case. But how to explain the phenomena to her gran?

"Isn't this wonderful?" Sue said looking around. "I wasn't sure it would work with just one earring."

"Oh Gran! You knew?"

"Of course, I knew! I wanted you to experience the past as I had done. Have you been to Whitehall Palace before?"

Lettie shook her head, trying to get her thoughts round the fact that her gran had known about the earrings and said nothing.

Sue marched across a torch lit courtyard towards a large square, single-story building. "Look there's Elizabeth's Banqueting Hall."

"Gran, slow down," Lettie called, heading towards the hall where a reception appeared to be taking place. "D'you think they'll let us in?" she asked, as they approached the entrance where a couple of liveried guards stood.

"We look the part, just ooze confidence."

They walked through the open doors without being challenged, into a large hall full of people dressed in exotic costumes. Lettie nudged her gran. "Why are they wearing masks and in fancy dress."

"It's probably a masquerade."

A gentleman in black, carrying a rod came towards them, bowed, and asked if he could assist them.

Sue inclined her head, "I am looking for my cousin the Countess of Essex."

"Ah, my lady is performing in the masquerade." He directed them to a space near a stage at the far end of the room.

The women on stage were performing in verse. Lettie watched for a while but found the hall more interesting than the play. It was very different to the present-day Banqueting Hall. Murals of exotic fruits and flowers decorated the walls which seemed to move in time with the music. She suddenly realised the walls weren't brick but painted canvas, supported on giant ship's masts, like a circus tent. Ivy was strung between the poles' and intertwined with garlands of fruits and flowers. Silver pendants, strung with golden grapes, hung from the ceiling, and glowed in the light from hundreds of glass lanterns. A grotto of magic, only not so magical when you saw the blue smoke haze collecting around the mast tops and each breath tasted of smoke.

A splash of crimson caught Lettie's eye, seated on a high-backed chair of gold and cherry red velvet, set under a canopy was Queen Elizabeth. Her gown of gold damask was decorated with gemstones and draped with strings of pearls. Lettie thought her the most striking woman in the hall. This was the real Virgin Queen, not a cinema creation. Elizabeth was speaking to a courtier who was perched on the edge of the plinth that raised her chair above the floor. He was entertaining her with much animation of his arms, the Queen laughed and clapped her hands. Lettie wished she could hear what he was saying.

The play finished and the audience began clapping. The Queen looked towards the stage and joined the applause.

"We must find the Countess," Sue said, tugging Lettie's hand.

"Gran, the Queen's over there, look!"

Sue was intent on pushing through the crowd. Lettie went to follow but a hand gripped her shoulder, turning her head she came face to face with Anne.

"I knew it was you! Come to spy on my Lord Leicester, have you?" Anne sneered, keeping a firm grip on Lettie.

"Please let go of me," Lettie murmured. "I'm not here to spy on anyone."

Anne was staring, wide eyed, at her necklace. "Where did you get that?" She lunged at Lettie taking her by surprise. Lettie felt the necklace's chain give way. The pendant bounced on the floor, split open and spilled out a folded scrap of paper.

"No!" Anne cried, diving after the pieces.

"What in God's name is going on here?" The Countess of Essex stared at Anne scrambling on the floor.

"She's a thief as well as a spy," Anne said, scooping up necklace pieces.

"Get up," the Countess hissed.

Anne got to her feet and furtively slid the scrap of paper into the folds of her gown.

Cat pointed at the broken necklace. "You told me you'd lost that in the grounds at Kenilworth. You were worried lest the Countess found it, as it's where you keep your secret admirer's love poem."

"Let me see." The Countess held out her palm and Anne placed the necklace in her hand. "And the poem."

Glaring at Cat, Anne dug in the folds of her skirt and produced the paper. The Countess unfolded the flimsy scrap and read it through, her colour rising. She read it a second time. "Where did you get this?"

Brushing dirt off her skirt, Anne mumbled, "It was handed to me, my lady."

"By whom?" The Countess tapped her foot. "I'm waiting."

"A groomsman, he said it was from an admirer."

"My son is no admirer of yours!"

Anne flushed, horrified. "Your son?"

Lettie whispered to her gran. "Anne thought the Earl of Leicester had sent the love poem."

"Really? Poor Anne."

"Gran, she's been a total bitch to me."

"Ah, I wonder if the young Earl of Essex was smitten with Anne or just playing a prank?"

Lettie thought for a moment. "She's so besotted with Leicester, I bet it never occurred to her that Essex had sent the poem, even though they're both called Robert."

"It's probably a good thing the Countess recognised her son's writing. At least it'll stop Anne making a fool of herself over Leicester."

One of the Countess's senior gentlewomen was escorting

Anne from the hall. She gave Lettie a venomous look.

The Countess's interest focused on Lettie. "When I first saw you at Kenilworth, I thought you were your grandmother," she laughed. "You are the image of her when we first met and that was a while ago. Do you remember, Susan?"

"It was here at Whitehall Palace. You were the Queen's Maid of Honour."

"Indeed." The Countess ran a critical eye over Lettie, "The family likeness is quite remarkable." She smiled, "Your grandmother has an uncanny way of appearing out of nowhere and it would seem you have also inherited this ability."

Lettie gave an uneasy laugh.

"Do you also have her gift for astrology?"

Lettie glanced at her gran, who gave a scant shake of the head. "My granddaughter's gifts lie in a different direction. She is an excellent dressmaker. As my gown testifies."

"To be sure, if your attire is a sample of her handiwork." The Countess studied the gown with an appreciative eye. "If I were to wear such a sumptuous creation, I'd rival my cousin, the Queen."

The musicians had struck up the first cords of a dance and Lettie watched the dancers assemble. The Queen was parading down the hall with the courtier who'd been sitting by her chair. Lettie turned to Cat. "Who is partnering the Queen?"

"Jean de Simier, emissary to the Duke d'Anjou," she replied. "They say the Queen will marry the Duke."

So that was Simier, Leicester's nemesis. The man he'd complained to Francis Knollys about. Lettie watched the Frenchman escort the Queen from the dance floor. As she reached her seat, Leicester arrived at her elbow and bent a knee. Elizabeth's face lit up in a warm smile, he offered her his arm and she placed her slender hand on his sleeve.

"A Galliard," the Countess observed as the music took on a lively tempo. "And Leicester must do his duty," she said, her voice tart.

Lettie exchanged a look with her gran. The Earl and Elizabeth took to the floor and in perfect harmony with the music they leapt, jumped, and hopped their way down the hall. Something they must have done hundreds of times before. The other dancers gave the couple the floor, applauding their performance. Lettie's eyes were on Simier. He was scowling at Leicester, even though he joined the applause.

The Countess turned her back on the dancers. "I must find my sister," she said, moving towards the exit.

"I must go too," Cat apologised. "Or I'll be in hot water with my lady."

Lettie slipped an arm through her gran's, who was eyeing up Leicester as he chatted with the Queen.

"Did you really read the Countess's stars?"

"Ah, well ... being pretty au fait with her life and knowing the Elizabethans' love of horoscopes. I fudged it."

"Gran! They'll think you're a witch!"

"I think they already do," she chuckled. Now I'd loved to read Leicester's palm," she said, looking across the hall. He had noticed their interest and was strolling towards them.

"Madam," He bowed to Sue, then considered Lettie for a moment, clearly trying to place her. "You're one of the Countess of Essex's women?"

"We are the Countess's cousins, Susan Fletcher, sir." She bobbed a curtsy. "And this—"

"Now I remember," Leicester frowned at Lettie. "You were in the garden at Wanstead, along with another of the Countess's women—"

"My lord," Sue cut in, "I do love the Courante, would you do me the honour of partnering me." Leicester's face was a picture of horror before his smooth courtly manners slid into place. "Of course, Madam."

Grateful for her gran's intervention, Lettie watched them join the other dancers then spotted Simier. He'd re-joined the Queen and was gesturing at Leicester. Elizabeth was getting angrier by the second. Splashes of scarlet appeared on her cheeks, enhanced by her white make-up.

"No, he would not dare!" The Queen leapt to her feet and strode towards Leicester. The other dancers retreated as she bore down on him. "Tell me it's not true!" She shrieked. Startled, Leicester let go of Sue's hand. The auditorium gasped and suddenly Elizabeth seemed to remember where she was. "Out, get out." Like sheep panicked by a wild dog, the revellers pushed for the exit.

Lettie stared at the Queen, struggling to take in what was happening. Elizabeth stood so close to Leicester she could have kissed him. Yet it was not love but fury in her eyes.

"Tell me it's not true," she challenged. "You would not dare marry that She Wolf without royal permission, would you?"

Leicester lowered his gaze. "I cannot deny that Lettice is my wife." He said softly reaching out to her. "Elizabeth!"

"The Devil take you," she spat, tears glittering in her eyes, "I'll see your head in a basket for this ... Guards! Where are the guards? My lord Leicester is to be confined in the Tower."

Sue backed away from them as the guards rushed forward. Simier had already fled.

"Gran, let's go," Lettie urged, grabbing her hand.

Outside, they stood in the shadows, ready to remove the pearl studs and depart the sixteenth century, when a movement in a gloomy doorway caught Lettie's eye. "Gran," she said softly, "isn't that Simier? And that's Cat with him." Without thinking, she marched into the torch lit square. "Cat are you okay?"

Cursing, Simier stepped aside to let Cat pass.

The girl hurtled toward her. "Oh Lettie!" she gasped. "He caught me as I came out the hall."

"Come off it, Cat. I saw you leave the hall well before him."

"Did I?"

"Yeah, you did." It dawned on her that Cat mightn't be the innocent she'd thought. Lettie glanced back at the doorway but Simier had vanished into the night. "Are you having an affair?"

Cat laughed. "What, with Simier? No. Ours is a business arrangement. Information. It's more profitable."

"You told him about the Countess's marriage."

"Don't pretend you're outraged," Cat said. "Anyway, all great houses have spies. If it hadn't been me then someone else would have reaped the profit. Simier is a useful friend."

"But what about the Countess?"

"She'll survive."

**

Back in the present-day Banqueting Hall Lettie and Sue headed for the bar.

"I don't know about you, but I could do with a drink," Sue said, eyeing up a tall barstool. Then deciding it would be too hazardous to clamber onboard in her gown. "My treat."

Lettie sipped the pink cocktail the bartender had put in front of her and pondered her latest trip into the past. The image she'd had in her head of Elizabeth I was somewhat different to the woman she'd seen. It wasn't difficult to understand why Leicester had wanted his marriage to remain a secret.

"That was delicious," Sue said, studying the raspberry-coloured dregs in her glass. "I think I'll have another, how about you?"

"Gran, did Elizabeth keep Leicester in the Tower for long?"

"Actually, he never went to the Tower. Elizabeth banished him from the Royal Court and made threatening noises, but he was still her favourite. She trusted and relied on him and in the end relented. The Countess wasn't so lucky. She was never allowed back at Elizabeth's court. The Queen could be vindictive when it came to her ladies. She took her displeasure out on the Countess by monopolising Leicester so he had very little time to spend with his wife."

Lettie considered this. "What happened to the child she was carrying?"

"There's no record of a baby, so probably she miscarried."

"Oh, that's sad."

"They did have a son, a year or so later."

"Well, that's something, at least. But I'm not sure I'm up for any more time travelling."

"Not even to become the Countess's dressmaker?"

"She did like the dress, didn't she? I'm surprised it didn't upset her, me copying her gown."

"Well, that's because the Countess of Essex's portrait you copied wasn't painted until about seven years after her marriage to Leicester." Sue grinned. "So, *she* pinched your design. Now do have another of these splendid cocktails."

ABOUT THE GROUPS

BROMLEY WRITERS

bromleywriters.wordpress.com

Run by Heather Johnston, the Bromley Writers are an inclusive group who meet every other Thursday evening above Bromley Library, though the sessions have converted to electronic form via Zoom for the time being. The group has been around for more than a decade with members from a range of backgrounds and experience, some of whom have found publication and competition success under Heather's guidance. The members explore a wide range of writing-related subjects during the sessions, and newcomers are always welcome to this friendly group, regardless of experience.

BRIXTON CREATIVE WRITING GROUP

With backing from AgeUK Lambeth's MySocial project, the Brixton Creative Writing Group was set up in 2017 by Ray Little, who has also been a member of the Bromley Writers for some years. In non-pandemic times, the friendly, fun sessions take place in the Vida Walsh Centre in Brixton, where the diversity and richness of South London is represented by its talented poets and writers. Scribblers of any age and experience are welcome, from complete beginner onwards. The lively sessions take place on alternate Thursdays to Bromley, though the past year has sadly kept the group apart physically, if not in spirit. Working on Journeys has kept the members in touch until the meet-ups can once again resume – bigger and better than ever.

ABOUT THE AUTHORS

ALISON BENNETT

Alison has been a craniosacral therapist for many years, and lives and works in Bromley. She mainly writes poetry and fiction, though she has also written short articles for local papers and specialist magazines. She worked as a technical writer for a couple of years, drawing on her experience as a (then) chartered accountant. For several years she was the administrator for the Ripley Poetry Association annual poetry competition.

Alison is currently writing poetry, a haiku diary, and a series of linked short stories with a supernatural theme. She has enjoyed working on the editorial side of the anthology as well as contributing to it.

FAY BROWN

Fay was born in London and has lived for most of her life in the inner city. She has a great empathy for people affected by stereotypes and social issues and through her writing challenges the status quo. She is inspired by her work with vulnerable and disadvantaged people through her extensive years of working in local government and the charity sector.

IAN D BROWN

Ian D. Brown was born and raised in London, where he still lives. He credits the inspiration behind his storytelling to the rich tapestry of London life and its myriad of characters. Ian's fascination with personality, dialogue, relationships and locale shines through in his writing style.

This is Ian's second publication, following the acclaimed and hard hitting 'The Un-Beautiful Game' which featured in the anthology 'South of the River'. Ian's ability to place the reader in the centre of a scene and submerge them in atmosphere is once again brought to the fore in this emotive tale, 'In the Symphony of Light'.

ANA CASTELLANI

Ana has poetry published in the anthologies Lost Things, Mad Like Us, and South of the River. Her work has existentialist and philosophical flavours, and is fuelled by a keen interest in neuroscience and psychology. When not travelling around the world to save the financial industry, Ana relaxes by watching TV, singing, dancing and driving around the gorgeous county of Kent.

RE CHARLES

Charles's autobiography, *Forty-Five Years of Always Being Right About Everything* was described as *'a moronic porridge of narcissism and self-aggrandisement'*, although he concedes the work also brought some negative reviews. His hobbies include making people jump and whistling loudly, and he is widely regarded as the man who coined the well-known phrases *'There's no place like Slough'* and *'Why can I never find a bloody pen in this house?'*

SUE EVANGELOU

Sue has attended and enjoyed several Creative Writing classes over the years. She has found that, in order to overcome her great ability for procrastination, she needs the discipline and encouragement that a class provides to enable her to actually sit down and write. Her current task is to record all the family stories that have been passed down to her so that, hopefully, future generations will find them of interest.

CLEO FELSTEAD

Cleo grew up in Middlesex and now lives in Kent with her partner and 4-year-old son. Always feeling freed by the pen, she flirts with the idea of writing on a regular basis and actually writes something occasionally. A full-time mum and part time children's DJ, Cleo spends a lot of time playing musical statues and splashing in muddy puddles.

TIA FISHER

Tia writes prose and poetry for both younger and older adults. Poems have previously been published in The Rialto magazine: she has won a TubeFlash competition and been longlisted for the MsLexia Children's Book Award. She is represented by the Eve White Literary Agency and her second YA narrative verse novel is currently on submission. Tia lives in Kent, where she deprives husband, cats and teenagers of attention in order to write.

TRISH GOMEZ

Trish lives in south London and enjoys the theatre, cinema, reading historical fiction and nonfiction and mystery novels. She has had success in a Woman's Weekly short story competition and has also had stories published in a magazine. The Time Traveller's Gown combines Trish's love of Tudor history with a touch of fantasy.

DOMINIC GUGAS

Dominic lives in Kent as the lone male with his wife, two daughters and two cats. He works in technology for a bank and spent much of his career designing call centres, which may make him one of the most evil beings on the planet. When he is not unleashing technological terrors on the public Dominic writes stories in the historical, fantasy, science fiction and "office weird" genres.

HC JOHNSTON

HC Johnston read English at Oxford University. A freelance business writer and consultant, with qualifications in economics and statistics, HCJ has run the Bromley Writers Group in association with Bromley Council Library Service since 2011.

Three one-act comedies performed professionally in London fringe theatres in 2007/8

Poetry: Commended, Brighton & Hove Poets, 2015

Short stories: 'Signature Dish' published in 'Tasting Notes', Ouen Press, 2018. 'Dogmeat' published in 'South of the River', Amazon, 2019. 'The Hoxton Particular', third prize, Exeter short story competition 2020, published on creativewritingmatters.co.uk.

'Charles and the Visitors', satirical novel, shortlisted for 2020 Exeter Prize

Monthly gardening column for local magazine, as 'Rose Green'

'From a Sussex Garden', gardening book, published Amazon, 2020

Current focus is on novels although if Mr. Spielberg wants some help, HCJ has play/screenwriting skills, and can be available.

RAYMOND LITTLE

Ray's short stories have appeared in numerous anthologies including the *Horror Library* series, and his story *The End of Science* was a Dark Tales prize winner. *An Englishman in St. Louis* sat alongside some of his own literary heroes such as Dickens, Poe and Conan Doyle in the *Chilling Ghost Short Stories* collection. Ray's debut novel, *Eyes of Doom*, was released by Blood Bound Books in 2017, and he was included in the Dead End Follies article *10 Brilliant Writers You Probably Don't Know*.

GWYNNETH PEDLER

Gwynneth Pedler was born in the East End of London in 1925, before moving to Maidenhead at the beginning of World War II and then later to Oxford, though she has now moved back to London to be near her two daughters. She had a long career in teaching, the last fifteen years as a head teacher. After retirement she went to Poland which had just achieved independence, to teach English for seven years, then to the same situation in Albania. These experiences have inspired much of her writing. Following a road traffic accident, she now relies on a wheelchair for mobility. She is well known for her ardent campaigning for equality, independence and accessibility. She loves children, cats, her garden and wearing bright-coloured clothes; dislikes pompous people.

MARGIT PHYSANT

Margit is retired, and an active campaigner for older people's issues. Since the pandemic she has rediscovered the joy of cycling. She is fond of the ancient Chinese proverb, "Every journey begins with a single step", which inspired this story.

SIOBHAN REARDON

Siobhan Reardon is a writer from Cork city, Ireland. She loves: The smell of gingerbread baking. Being near the sea. The way swallows fling themselves on the air in early summer. The blue haze of a bluebell wood in Spring. And reading Dickens' Christmas stories in the 'wee small hours' of a winter morning. She loves the word 'gregarious' because she is! And her favourite word is 'Wanderlust' because it is a bold word, and powerful - and perhaps a little poignant right now.

LORAINE SAACKS

Loraine Saacks was born in London a few days after Pearl Harbour was attacked in 1941. First years in Sidcup, Kent – and the Chislehurst Caves, dodging bombs, overnight. Worked on the Editorial Floor of the *Sunday Mirror* and much later *Woman's Journal* in past years. Having been re-booted as an au pair, for late arrival of a flurry of grandchildren, has now been made redundant, as charges are now towering over her. Recent work published in Mslexia, Live Canon and shortlisted in first twenty of Writers and Artists Year Book's short story competition, in 2016. Now trying to complete a spoof play, centred on the Cuba Crisis which lasted from 16th October to 28th October 1962 – in time for its Diamond Anniversary in 2022.

CAROLE TYRRELL

Carole Tyrrell has been a member of the Bromley Writers Group since it began. She enjoys writing ghost stories, the odd piece of speculative fiction and book reviews. Welcome Aboard was inspired by her seeing a train stop at a station one weekend when they weren't supposed to be running, and wondering what would have happened if she'd boarded. Carole also has a surreal sense of humour which keeps her going in life.

Carole's stories have appeared in *The Silent Companion, Ghosts & Scholars, Revelation, Siren's Call* and *Supernatural Tales*. She has also published a non-fiction piece on *Medium*. In addition, she has been published in 4 anthologies: *South of the River, Brainbox, The Ghosts and Scholars Book of Folk Horror* and the *Ghosts & Scholars Book of Mazes*.

Carole has enjoyed being part of the editorial team as editing is often where a story can take shape and its themes emerge.

ROBERT WILLIAMS

Robert lives in Bromley and earns his living as a software engineer. He would much rather be a writer, an occupation that is much more fun but pays badly, if at all.

He had two stories published in South of the River about the adventures of an urban witch called Mags. For *Journeys*, he has provided two science fiction stories, but he will be returning to writing more *Tales of an Urban Witch* when the *Journeys* project has finished.

Robert was delighted to be asked to help edit *Journeys* and has really enjoyed seeing this volume develop over the last few months.

THE PRODUCTION TEAM

ROBERT WILLIAMS
*Prose Edits, Content compilation,
Layout and Cover Design*

ALISON BENNETT
Poetry and Prose Edits

CAROLE TYRRELL
Prose Edits

RAY LITTLE
Poetry and Prose Edits, Concept

BOOKS IN THIS SERIES

SOUTH OF THE RIVER

The series contains the collected creative work from writing groups in Brixton and Bromley.

South Of The River

South of the River is the first collection of the best fiction and poetry from the Brixton and Bromley creative writing groups. Some authors were previously published, others are showcasing their work here for the first time, but they all have one thing in common; imagination. Romance, history, murder, sci-fi, sex and horror - it is all here in this marvellous collection.

Printed in Great Britain
by Amazon